"Damn It, Andrea,"

he began in a rare show of temper.

"Andy to you," she snapped, interrupting him swiftly. "*No one* calls me Andrea."

He caught her shoulders, suddenly furious that she could refuse the gift of her own femininity. "Well, someone should! Maybe then you'd realize you're a woman instead of a truck-driving female." He snatched his hands away to jam them into his pockets. He'd shake her if he touched her for one second longer. "You'd be a beautiful, sexy creature a man would be proud to be seen with if you'd ever quit emulating your brother and your father."

Andrea drew back as if he had slapped her. "What right have you got to question my actions? I've seen you exactly four times in my life, and every one of them began and ended just like this." She stabbed a finger at his chest. "I *am not* copying anyone. I'm doing what I like. So get off my case."

Dear Reader,

Welcome to Silhouette! Our goal is to give you hours of unbeatable reading pleasure, and we hope you'll enjoy each month's six new Silhouette Desires. These sensual, provocative love stories are both believable and compelling—sometimes they're poignant, sometimes humorous, but always enjoyable.

Indulge yourself. Experience all the passion and excitement of falling in love along with our heroine as she meets the irresistible man of her dreams and together they overcome all obstacles in the path to a happy ending.

If this is your first Desire, I hope it'll be the first of many. If you're already a Silhouette Desire reader, thanks for your support! Look for some of your favorite authors in the coming months: Stephanie James, Diana Palmer, Dixie Browning, Ann Major and Doreen Owens Malek, to name just a few.

Happy reading!

Isabel Swift
Senior Editor

SDRL-7/85

SARA CHANCE
Where the Wandering Ends

Silhouette Desire

Published by Silhouette Books New York

America's Publisher of Contemporary Romance

For the real Big Jack and his wife, Pat.
You raised my brother and I and opened your heart
and home to other children who needed a family.
Thank you for being the people you are.

SILHOUETTE BOOKS
300 East 42nd St., New York, N.Y. 10017

Copyright © 1987 by Sydney Ann Clary

ISBN: 0-373-05357-6

First Silhouette Books printing June 1987

America's Publisher of Contemporary Romance

Printed in the U.S.A.

SARA CHANCE,

"wife, mother, author, in that order," currently resides in Florida with her husband. With the ocean minutes from her door, Ms. Chance enjoys both swimming and boating.

A whisper on the wind calls to me
Beckoning me onward to the mysterious far horizon
Alone, I search for I know not what
My arms are empty, my heart untouched
Where does my lover wait for me?

One

Andrea froze, her gaze searching around the shadowy form of her eighteen-wheeler. There was someone hiding nearby. The sound of breathing was faint but unmistakable. She took a better grip of the big flashlight she carried before angling her head to see if Jo-Jo had come out of the rest room yet. The sight of his bulky silhouette heading toward her was comforting. A rasp from beneath her truck drew her attention.

"What's wrong, Andy?" Jo-Jo rumbled as he joined her.

"There's someone under the rig," she whispered.

"You're joking. Only a fool would try something in this rest stop." The older man bent slightly to peer under the semi. "Who'd wanna be skulking around here?" he continued, making no effort to lower his voice. He pulled Andrea's light from her fingers and shone it beneath the frame. "I'll be— It's a kid." He hunched down to get a better look. "At least, I think so."

Andrea glanced around the well-lit parking area, seeing no other vehicle but their two tractor trailers. "It can't be," she muttered, stooping to stare under her cab. "There aren't any other cars here, and there sure aren't any houses near this stretch of interstate."

Jo-Jo ignored her comment as he thrust the flashlight at her. "Hold this while I see if I can get the little fella out," he directed, edging closer. "Come on out, son; we won't hurt you." He waited patiently for a response.

Andrea frowned while the silence lengthened. "Maybe you ought to go in after him," she suggested finally.

Jo-Jo glanced up, his teeth flashing in a brief grin. "If I do, he's only going to scoot out in another direction."

"So, we'll just catch him," she replied, seeing no problem. At least he would be out in the open.

Her companion chuckled at her seemingly logical answer. "It's easy to tell you don't know anything about children."

"No, I don't," she agreed readily, "but with three of your own, you do. So do something. Marge is expecting you by midnight, and you know how she worries when you're late. Besides, I'm tired. I've been pushing all day to get home myself.''

"Okay, okay.'' Jo-Jo shook his dark head. "Just don't say I didn't warn you.'' He crawled under the front bumper to reach for the child huddled near the middle of the tractor. He swore loudly a moment later before beating a hasty retreat.

"What's wrong?'' Andrea demanded when he came up nursing his right hand. She shone the light on his pain-contorted features.

"The little devil bit me.'' He displayed a semicircular wound showing faint drops of red.

Dumbfounded, Andrea stared at him blankly. "We can't leave him there. And I sure can't move the truck,'' she stated, voicing the obvious.

Jo-Jo dug into his pocket for his handkerchief, then tied it over his injury. "Tell you what, you watch the kid and I'll go radio for a 'bear.' I think I saw one parked by that airline billboard six miles back.''

Andy caught his arm, stopping him before he could move away. "Unless they've changed the duty roster a week early, that smokey'll be McMann. And you know what a pain he is,'' she reminded him. None of the drivers on this route liked the state trooper and Andy was no exception. She wouldn't have handed her worst enemy over to the man, much less a child, no matter how troublesome he was.

Jo-Jo grimaced, his expression conveying his own dislike of the officious highway patrolman who was such a stickler for regulations. "Damn,'' he groaned.

"Why don't you try it again?" she whispered. "I'll distract him and you grab him."

He hesitated, glaring first at Andrea's rig, then at Andrea herself. "Watch his teeth," he warned before getting into position again.

Andrea touched the sleeve of her chocolate-colored suede jacket. "I doubt if his bite could penetrate this stuff," she pointed out, squatting down. For the first time, she got a good look at the child hiding under her rig. Great scared eyes stared at her out of a thin, fear-whitened face. He was little more than a dirt-smeared youngster.

"Good Lord," she breathed with an unexpected surge of admiration at the defensive yet courageous way he confronted her. Gutsy little boy. Barely conscious of the stream of soothing words escaping her lips, she moved forward. His eyes were green, she realized, as she finally got within touching distance. "Give me your hand," she commanded softly, gentling him, she hoped, with her tone.

He shook his head, his gaze never leaving hers. He squirmed back an inch, unknowingly bringing his body within easy reach of Jo-Jo's outstretched hands.

In that second, Hades exploded around Andrea. Jo-Jo let out a howl of pain as the boy sank his teeth into his wrist. Their quarry somehow skinned out of the small area and made a break for the dim fringes of the rest stop. Andy slithered out and was in hot pursuit without even thinking about it. Her long legs stretched in a fluid stride as she ate up the child's lead. She was a pace behind him when he crashed to a halt at the fence boundary. He whirled to face her, his bony frame shuddering with the effort he'd expended.

"That's it," Andrea snapped, propping her hands on her denim-clad hips. "I've had enough. Now Jo-Jo's told you and I've told you we're *not* going to hurt you. I'm too blasted tired to go chasing you around all night. And I doubt that Jo-Jo's willing to offer you any more hands to chew on." She glared at the young culprit before gesturing toward her eighteen-wheeler. "That's my rig." She pointed to the other semi a few yards away. "That's my friend, Jo-Jo's, down there. Now I'm going to get in my truck and I'm going home. There's a room there, food and a bed that you can use if you want. I'm not going to force you to come with me. But I'll tell you, staying out here in the dark will be uncomfortable and cold without any more clothes on than you have."

She waited, knowing she was probably handling the whole situation all wrong. What did she know about children? That was her brother, Ray's, and his wife's specialty. She didn't even have a dog because she was never in one place long enough to take the responsibility.

"Well, are you coming or not?" she demanded when he still didn't speak. From the corner of her eye she monitored Jo-Jo's cautious approach.

The boy caught the movement, and in a flash threw himself at Andrea's legs, clinging to her with surprising strength. It was a toss-up as to who was the most shocked of the three.

"Likes you better'n me," Jo-Jo observed in undisguised surprise, scratching his head. "Whatcha gonna do with him?"

Andy stared down at the small body pressed against her. For a second she had a strong urge to smooth the tangled dark curls in comfort. "Take him home, like I said," she murmured, wondering what she was doing, offering, much less intending, to do it.

Irritated at herself for getting involved, she caught the boy's shoulders to unplaster him from her body. He fought her for a moment but he refrained from using his teeth.

"What's your name?" she asked the instant she pried him loose.

He shook his head but otherwise stood still. Ray would know what to do, she assured herself. She'd turn her charge over to him and Faith. Suddenly assailed by a horrible thought, Andrea's violet eyes narrowed. "Can you talk?" She groaned aloud when she received another shake in answer.

Jo-Jo swore roughly. "I don't like this, Andy. We'd better get the patrol."

At the mention of the law officer, the child began to renew his squirming for freedom.

"Dammit, Jo-Jo, shut up," Andrea snapped, picking up her reluctant passenger and tucking him, kicking and struggling, under one arm.

"Don't yell at me, Andrea Carpenter. You know damned well I'm right," he retaliated in an annoyed roar. He strode beside her to her truck.

She stopped beside her rig, ignoring her burden's weakening attempts to escape. "Right now, I'm not interested in anyone's rights except this child's and mine. His skin is like ice, he's dirty, scared and probably hungry and tired. And, leaving out the first three, I'm not feeling too good-natured, either. So—" she turned and opened the passenger door with her free hand "—I'm going home and I'm taking him with me. Ray can sort out the legalities of this mess and he can contact the authorities. He's a lawyer and his home is a juvenile emergency shelter. It won't be the first time he's been involved in this kind of a problem."

She lifted her charge up. "Put your feet on the rungs," she directed, referring to the small indentations in the side of the elevated cab to allow easy entry. When the boy obediently did as he was told, she released him and he scrambled up onto the seat. "Don't touch *anything*. I'm going to shut the door, walk around and get in on the other side. Nod if you understand."

He dipped his head, his eyes darting from her to Jo-Jo's scowling face. "He's not coming, don't worry," she reassured him hurriedly, dreading another tussle. With her words, he slumped in his seat as though suddenly every ounce of fight had drained out of him.

"I'll be a flat tire," Jo-Jo muttered, making no secret of his amazement. "The little devil's listening to you."

Andrea slammed the tractor door, privately as stunned as Jo-Jo at the child's strange attachment to her. "He knows I'm not going to take any sass," she offered, vaguely remembering one of her father's favorite sayings.

An unintelligible grunt was her friend's answer to her attempted explanation. "Front door or back?" she queried as she halted beside her truck. The CB slang slipped out as she turned her attention to business.

"Back," he replied. "You're leaving the interstate first so I might as well follow you. Besides, if you have any trouble, it'll be easier for me to stop and help."

Andy grinned and patted his arm affectionately. Jo-Jo was a good friend and only slightly older than her oldest brother, Ray. He had been driving trucks for as long as she had, and this was far from the first time they had traveled the road together.

"Don't worry. I think he's too exhausted to give a mouse a problem now," she pointed out, mounting up.

Jo-Jo shut her door, his expression lightening slightly. "I can't wait to tell Marge about this," he commented, a suspicion of suppressed amusement in his voice. He chuckled openly at her annoyed glare before strolling toward his truck.

Andrea watched him go, knowing that by morning half the state's truckers would know about her quixotic impulse. She was definitely in for at least a week or two of ribbing over this night's work. She scowled briefly as she switched on the big engine. She cast her passenger a swift look to find his gaze riveted on the various dials and gauges lining the dash panel.

The expression of awe on his face would have amused her at another time but not tonight. She had to be out of her mind, she berated herself silently while she guided her rig back onto the interstate. She had saddled herself with a child without knowing one single thing about him. Right now his people could be searching for him. She should have let Jo-Jo get the trooper, but for some stupid reason, she hadn't been able to tolerate the thought of this boy spending the night in some strange place while he waited for someone to come for him.

"Breaker, breaker. You got your ears on, Purple Flash?"

Andy lifted the CB mike to her mouth to answer Jo-Jo's call, stifling a sigh at the fleeting flicker of apprehension the intrusion had caused in the boy beside her.

"Gotcha, Snowball, come on back," she replied before releasing the talk button. "It's only the radio," she soothed, not liking the fear on the child's face. No one that small and defenseless should look like that. Dividing her glance between him and the road, she barely heard Jo-Jo's voice. It was more important that her reluctant passenger relax.

"Hey, Flash, you got cotton in your ears?" Jo-Jo's demand rose above the level of his usual cheerful chatter.

Andrea sighed, vaguely annoyed at her concern over the child's reactions. "I'm here," she shot back, barely managing to keep the edge out of her tone. "Let's cut the gab. It's scaring the boy."

A moment later the CB went silent once more. Andrea shifted in her plush seat, restless and uneasy with the whole situation. Absently, she noted the mile marker on her right. Twenty more to go and she would be almost home. And rid of her responsibility, of her impulsive action, she added silently.

A small, grubby hand hesitantly touched her sleeve, drawing her attention. She followed the direction of the pointing finger, accurately reading the question in the solemn green eyes staring at her.

"Pressure gauges," she answered the unspoken query slowly. The finger found another target. "AM-FM stereo radio. Air conditioning controls for the tractor. Fuzz buster." She laughed at the puzzled look on the boy's face at the strange name before going on to explain. "A radar detection device. It tells me if a bear—highway patrol to you—is tracking my speed with a radar machine."

"You need a name," she said abruptly, her brow wrinkling in thought. "I can't keep on calling you nothing. A scrapper like you has to have a handle." She glanced at him, catching the faint trace of pleasure at her description. "Like that, do you?" she said, grinning, privately glad the problem was so easily solved. "Scrapper, it is then." She hesitated, giving him a quick dark look. "But only if you promise no biting, kicking or scratching. 'Cause I'll turn you over my knee if you lay your teeth into me, my boy."

Scrapper shook his head vigorously. He crossed his heart in a child's symbolic promise.

Relieved, Andrea relaxed. She leaned over to switch on her favorite country station. The sounds of "Alabama" filled the cab, eliminating any further need for communication. She exited the interstate a short time later, deciding to head for home instead of the yard. Pop wouldn't care and it sure wasn't the first time a rig had occupied the driveway of their home. She eased carefully along her street, gearing down as quietly as possible to avoid disturbing their few, widely spaced neighbors.

The sight of Ray's car in the main drive was especially welcome. Now she would have some expert help with her passenger. Not only was Ray a good lawyer, but he and his wife, had two boys of their own. Best of all, between Ray's volunteer work at Springfield's boy's club once a month and his experience as a shelter parent, he would know exactly how to handle the child. She killed the motor before leaping down to the ground. She walked to the front of the truck, expecting to meet Scrapper there.

"Come on down," she commanded, going around to his side. She opened his door to find him scooting as far out of reach as he could get. "Not again? I thought we settled this habit of yours earlier," she muttered, climbing wearily back into the cab. She stared into his frightened face, swearing inwardly at his attitude. "I'm not going to drop you off. I live here, too. Right down there in that small house." She pointed to a clearly visible path leading toward a group of shadowed trees. "My brothers and my father are in the big house. You'll like them. They're truckers, too,'' she added, stretching the truth a bit. She held out her hand. "Let's go. I'm anxious to get home even if you aren't." She waited, unconsciously holding her breath.

Seconds ticked by as he watched her. Then slowly, gingerly, he laid his fingers in hers. Andrea sighed, unexpectedly pleased at the tiny flicker of trust shining in his eyes. She couldn't remember the last time she had worked so hard for so little. Together they headed for the house. There was no noticeable hesitation other than the tightening of Scrapper's grip on her hand as they crossed the small hall and entered the living room.

Andrea paused on the threshold, momentarily surprised at the number of people in the room—her father, Ray and Faith and a visitor who had a familiar look about him. Impatiently she dismissed the unknown, turning instead to her older brother.

"Ray, you're just the man I need," she announced, striding forward with Scrapper at her side. "My friend here has a problem that needs sorting out."

Ray's expression reflected his astonishment at this bit of news. "Friend?" he queried, staring first at her, then at the child whose hand she held.

"Yes, friend," she stated firmly, visually daring him to comment on the improbability of her arriving with a child in tow. Idiot. Any fool could see the boy was in some kind of a fix. Now wasn't the time to be worried about her involvement.

"Who is he?" the visitor asked, interrupting without compunction.

Andrea turned, ready to demand what business it was of his when recognition dawned. Only one man she knew had that upper crust Boston accent, tinged with a liquid smoothness.

"Nicholas Griffin," she breathed, her eyes surveying him in barely concealed surprise. "The last time I saw you was three years ago." It wouldn't even have been then if she could have avoided it, she amended silently. She had been on one of her rare stopovers and he had been visiting Ray and Faith.

He inclined his head, the light gleaming briefly over the rich mahogany of his stylishly cut hair. "You haven't changed much since your high school graduation," he murmured, his gaze roaming over her short cropped, black curls and slender frame.

Andrea caught the unmistakable, though habitual, disapproval in his blue-green eyes before they finally rested on Scrapper. She stiffened at his response, remembering the chance remark she had overheard all those years ago. More boy than girl, he had said. A devastating statement to make about any young female. But hardly important now, she reminded herself, deliberately relaxing once more. That was the past and this was the present. Now, Scrapper needed help.

"So who's your friend?" Nick repeated, bending down so that he was at eye level with Scrapper.

The child pressed against Andrea, his body going rigid. Without thinking, Andrea put an arm around his shoulders to hug him to her side. "Back up. Can't you see you're scaring him?" she snapped before turning to glare at Ray. "I picked him up at the last rest stop," she began, quickly outlining the events of the evening. All the time she spoke Scrapper huddled against her. "So, since I couldn't go on thinking of him as the kid, he's been dubbed Scrapper temporarily." She stopped, giving him an encouraging smile. She studiously ignored Nick's faint expression of surprise when the boy's lips curved slightly in return.

"I'm proud of you, Andy," Big Jack Carpenter interposed heartily, speaking for the first time. "Who knows what could have happened to the mite if you hadn't come along?"

"You should have notified the troopers, you know," Ray pointed out, his lawyer's mind making itself felt.

"I agree," Nick added, lending the weight of his own legal training to his friend's opinion.

Andrea glared at them. "If you'd have seen how scared he was, you'd have done just what I did," she denied vigorously.

"I agree with Andy," Faith and Big Jack spoke together, ranging themselves wholeheartedly on her side.

"The point is what do we do?"

Ray sighed while exchanging a look with Nick. "I'll call the authorities. Right now Faith and I don't have any children staying with us so maybe we can keep Scrapper for the time being." He turned to his father. "That is, if you don't mind one more house guest while we're waiting on the decorators to finish our place."

Big Jack shook his head. "No problem, son. You know I've got plenty of room. Ned and I rattle around in this old barn all by ourselves. It's nice to have company for a change.''

Andrea glanced down to the child she protected. "Okay, Scrapper, you'll stay here with Big Jack, Ray, Faith and me.'' He nodded, clinging to her with all his strength. Andrea carefully detached his fingers before going down on her knees in front of him. "Now, I'm going to leave you with Faith and she'll put you to bed with her boys. I'll be down to my house so I can sleep, then I'll see you in the morning.'' He began to shake his head vehemently from side to side, his expression tightening with apprehension.

"Stop that,'' Andrea commanded impatiently. "You promised, remember? I can't take you with me because I don't have any place for you to sleep.'' She caught his shoulders to still his jerky movements. "I...want...you...to...stay...here,'' she directed, spacing her words carefully. "You can see my rig from your window. I couldn't leave here without it and, if I tried, the sound of the motor would waken you.'' She waited, silently hoping he would accept her assurances.

Slowly she felt his tension ease, the terror leave his eyes until finally he gave a small nod of agreement. Andrea rose, took his hand and led him to Faith. The sympathy in her sister-in-law's brown eyes was reassuring.

"How about if we go by way of the kitchen and scrounge some food and hot chocolate and stuff?'' said Faith, as she and Scrapper left the room. Andrea watched them go, certain she would see the child's look of trust in her mind for a long time to come.

"I never would have believed you had it in you, Andrea Carpenter," Nick murmured softly for her ears alone.

Two

"Slow down, Andrea," Nick commanded, catching her arm.

Andy halted abruptly while at the same time shrugging out of his hold. "It was *your* idea to see me to my door," she countered with marked sarcasm. "I don't *need* your escort and what's more, I don't want it. I'm perfectly capable of crossing a hundred yards or so of our own land even if it's almost midnight." She glared at him, making no secret of her irritation at his presence. The darkness hid most of her expression, but she didn't care. Nick disapproved of her and always had. In fact, he was probably her least favorite male in the long list of those she knew in her masculine dominated field.

"Dammit, Andrea," he began in a rare show of temper.

"Andy to you," she snapped, interrupting him swiftly. "*No one* calls me Andrea."

He caught her shoulders, suddenly furious that she could refuse the gift of her own femininity. "Well, someone should! Maybe then you'd realize you're a woman instead of a truck driving female." He snatched his hands away to jam them into his pockets. He'd shake her if he touched her for one second longer. "You'd be a beautiful, sexy creature a man would be proud to be seen with if you'd ever quit emulating your brother, Ned, and your father."

Andrea drew back as if he had slapped her. "What right have you got to question my actions? I've seen you exactly four times in my life and every one of them began and ended just like this." She stabbed a finger at his chest. "I *am not* copying anyone. I'm doing what I like. I grew up around trucks. I played in my dad's yard with mechanics for babysitters while you were going to all those proper schools. Sure, I run the roads, but I know darned near every trucker and his family on this whole east coast. Some of them are as close to me as my own father and my brothers. I'm safer and better protected than I'd be as a secretary in a city like Boston, New York or Los Angeles. So get off my case." She whirled around, her anger expended, to stride down the path toward her house.

"Overbearing stuffed shirt," she muttered under her breath. "Self-righteous prig." She gritted her teeth as every step she took had a heavier echo in one of

Nick's paces. "Go on back, Mr. Fancy-suited Lawyer," she commanded without turning around. "I'm tough, remember. No self-respecting attacker would dare tackle me."

"I'm going to make sure you're all right," he bit out, making no effort to alter his speed to either catch up or let her go.

Andrea saw the small shape of her cottage with a mixture of relief and regret. Relief that she would be rid of her self-appointed guardian and regret that she hadn't thought of some pithy comment to alter his unbelievably twisted opinion of her. But then, what did she care what he thought? she reminded herself as she inserted her key in the lock and opened the door. She reached inside to switch on the lights before facing him.

"Thanks for protecting me from the boogie men," she simpered sweetly, knowing she was behaving badly but not really caring. Somehow Nick always managed to bring out the worst in her, even when she had only been a tomboyish teenager.

"Andrea Carpenter, you'd try the patience of an angel."

"And you're not that," she snapped, preparing to defend herself. She nearly disgraced her image by gasping when, with a heavy sigh, Nick turned on his heel and strode back the way they had come. "Well, I'll be..." she mumbled, watching him head toward the house where he would be spending the night. It was the first time he had ever let her have the last word. For a moment, she stood on her porch recalling the surprisingly vivid memories of their earlier encounters.

Their initial meeting had been when she was fourteen and he was a freshman in college, spending his first weekend with her family. She had come home from the playground after rescuing a friend's cat from a tree. She had been dirty, her blouse and jeans bearing the marks of her climb and her cheek scratched from a branch. She had looked as grubby as Scrapper and, with her short hair, almost as boyish. And Nick's expression had conveyed his surprise and unflattering amusement.

A year later he had been a witness to her first and only attempt at motocross. He hadn't laughed then, as she recalled. In fact, thinking back, he had acted furious.

But perhaps the most memorable meeting had been at the graduation party her family had given her. As a friend of Ray's, Nick had been included. He had escorted a gorgeous redhead who had been a classmate of his and Ray's. His date had been everything she wasn't and doubted she ever could be. And she had been angry, unreasonably so. But the cap for her evening had been when one of the boys had shown his ardor by cornering her in the garden. His determined pursuit, terminating in an unwanted, intimate kiss, had won him a stinging slap. Her aim had been good and his balance none too steady. He had landed with a resounding plop right at Nicholas's and his companion's feet. It was later that Andrea had overheard Nick talking to her brother, Ned.

"More boy than girl," she mumbled, easily recalling the disgust and disapproval in his tone. Andrea padded through her living room to her bedroom, barely glancing at the surprisingly feminine decor done in shades of her favorite lavender and purple. She shed her clothes, admitting she had consciously avoided Nick on his occasional visits with Ray and her family. Usually it was simple because she was almost always on the road.

She showered and slid naked between soft violet-sprinkled sheets. If it hadn't been for Faith's sudden spate of home redecorating, painting and wallpapering, she would've missed her nemesis this time, too. Sighing at the fact that she was stuck with him this weekend, she closed her eyes and willed her body to relax. Blast Nicholas Griffin and his antiquated ideas, she muttered as, inevitably, exhaustion claimed her and she slept.

Seconds later—or was it hours—the phone shrilled beside her bed. She jerked awake to grope for the receiver. Faith's tearful voice brought her completely alert and she heard a howl of pain in the background.

"Surely you've dealt with nightmares before," Andrea argued, totally at a loss after her sister-in-law's explanation.

Faith ignored her comment if she even heard it. "He barricaded himself in the corner of the living room. He's got an arsenal of things to throw if anyone gets too close and he's bitten the men every time they try to get near him. My boys are up and getting a ringside seat, too," she added as a concerted yell of "Get him" sounded in the background.

"I'll be right over," Andrea decided tersely. She hung up without waiting for a reply while simultaneously sliding out of bed. She slipped into her jeans and socks in a rush, pausing only long enough to put on her suede zip-up jacket for a top. She refused to waste seconds hunting for her shirt. Intending to pick up her boots where she usually left them by the front door, she hurried through the house. They weren't there.

"Fiddle," she groaned. She cast one quick glance around, then decided she could do without them. Her socks would protect her feet. Leaving the lights on in the house, she started down the path at a trot. She stumbled slightly as she hit the first rock. The second drew a wince, the third a mumbled curse which grew louder with every obstacle after that. By the time she limped her way to her destination, her temper was shot.

Chaos reigned as she entered the living room. Four grown men in various kinds of night apparel formed a wary semi-circle around a large chair. She could barely make out Scrapper's small head behind the barrier as a figurine came lobbing over the furniture at Ned's slowly advancing form.

"Damn," he swore as he dodged swiftly to one side.

Andrea strode forward, ignoring the missile-littered floor. "Now you stop that right now, you little devil," she commanded, wading in between Ned's stocky frame and Ray's more lightweight body. She pinned her charge with a glare. "If I'd have wanted my home destroyed, I'd have hired somebody to do it," she added irritably as she reached her quarry. Scrapper stared up at her, visibly subdued by her annoyance.

She held out her hand. "Give me that vase." He glanced at the line of adults behind her, then at the makeshift weapon. He shook his head and backed up a step.

Andrea sighed frustratedly before running her fingers through her disheveled hair. She could yank him out of his hole simply enough, disarm him, too, if she had to. But she hated to do it. The fine tremors beneath the oversized T-shirt he wore worried her.

No one else in the room moved or made a sound as the boy and the woman stared at each other, locked in a battle of wills. Andrea faced her small adversary, wishing she knew what she was doing. How did a person go about reasoning with a child? Mothers did it all the time; she'd seen Faith in action with her own offspring.

"I'll go upstairs and stay with you until you sleep," she tried hopefully. He shook his head without relaxing at all. Andrea racked her brain for a solution, but the only thing she could come up with was hardly a good alternative. "Do you want to sleep at the cottage with me?" she asked, resigned to her fate.

Scrapper gazed at her, his eyes begging for reassurance that she really meant what she said.

Andrea extended her hand. "Come on," she commanded quietly.

Slowly he lowered his makeshift missile to the cushion on the floor at his feet. Then, so quickly that he caught her by surprise, he grabbed her fingers in a tight, two-fisted grip. Andrea lifted him up and over his fortress. She could almost feel the collective sigh of relief as she turned around.

Somehow without meaning to, her eyes sought Nick's lean form. His bare-chested body made little impression for it was his expression that held her momentarily motionless. Admiration, approval, plus a hefty measure of amazement were written clearly in his finely honed features.

"Now, maybe we can get some sleep," Ned mumbled as he bent to pick up one of his nephews.

Ray nodded, a faint grin curving his mouth. "I'll second that." He tucked an arm around Faith's waist to lead her, with their youngest in her arms, out of the room. Ned followed them, leaving behind Big Jack.

"Sorry about this, Pop," Andrea apologized.

Her parent chuckled good-naturedly, looking anything but annoyed at his interrupted sleep. His dark gray eyes scanned the miniature warlord at her side. "Forget it, Andy. Parts of this evening have been very interesting. You've got a good arm, son. Get Andy to show you how to pitch at the tire hanging from the old oak tree tomorrow. It's a much better target than aiming at my boys." With that suggestion, he inclined his iron-gray head and walked toward the door without another word.

"Let's go," Nick suggested, moving toward her.

"Go?" she questioned blankly, staring at him. "Go where?"

"To your cottage. Scrapper's going to need a coat. That T-shirt's too skimpy for a walk in the cool night air."

"I know that," Andrea responded defensively. "I was going to give him mine." With her free hand, she started to unzip her jacket only to stop abruptly when she remembered what she didn't have on. She glanced up to find Nick watching her with unabashed curiosity. "You could've reminded me," she muttered self-consciously.

He laughed softly, enjoying her unusual distraction. For the first time since he had known her, he was aware of her as a woman. She still wasn't his idea of femininity, but she did have a certain earthy appeal, he decided, his gaze lingering briefly on the gentle swell of her breasts visible above the opening of her jacket. Just for a second he wondered what color her eyes would be when they were clouded with passion—a soft morning-tinted violet or perhaps the deep, mysterious purple velvet of the night?

"Stop staring at me," Andrea murmured with restrained force. If she were the blushing type, she'd have been covered in a pink flush by now.

"Sorry," he replied with a shrug, willing his mind to cease its fruitless fantasizing. Of all the females he could have picked, Andrea was without a doubt the least appealing to him personally. He liked his women beautiful, intelligent and secure in their own femininity. Andrea, in his opinion, was doing her best to minimize her natural gifts and deny her own sex.

"You don't need to walk with us," she began.

"I know you'd rather take care of yourself, but for once consider another point of view." He glanced significantly at the drooping child beside her. "You might need an extra pair of hands before you get home."

Andrea hesitated, oddly tempted to accept his offer. Yet why should she? She was capable of carrying Scrapper if she had to. She opened her lips to refuse only to be stopped by the challenging glint in his eyes.

"All right," she agreed finally. She started for the hall without waiting to see his reaction. He was right beside her to lend his assistance in getting Scrapper into one of her old jackets, which was still hanging in the closet by the front door.

Glancing briefly at his bare torso, she reached inside the narrow compartment once more. "You'd better take this," she said, removing Ned's favorite heavy plaid shirt from a hanger.

One dark brow quirked upward at her less than gracious tone of voice, although he made no comment. He slipped into the red-and-navy flannel, ignoring the fact he could have wrapped it around himself twice.

Unable to help herself, Andrea watched him put on Ned's shirt, unconsciously enjoying the smooth rhythm of his movements. Even the overlarge effect of his attire did nothing to hide the swordlike leanness of his body. Her gaze lifted to his face to catch the carefully blank mask over his features. Suddenly the incongruity of their respective states of dress, the late hour and the battle that had brought them to this moment struck her funny.

She tried and failed to stifle the laughter bubbling within her. "It's a good thing Ned still shares the house with Pop," she managed, attempting to disguise her amusement with words. "Pop's things would look even more like a tent on you."

Stung by what he thought was criticism, Nick glared at her. He may not be built along the lines of a football player like most of her family, but he was no lightweight either. "Don't start, Andrea," he drawled, irritated. "It's late and I'm too d—" he bit back the swear word he had intended "—tired to fight with you." He turned to open the door, gesturing her through with a curt wave of his hand.

Shocked by his sudden show of temper, Andrea obeyed him automatically. She and Scrapper descended the porch steps together as she pondered how she could have annoyed him. She had only been teasing after all.

"Whatever it was I said, I take it back," she offered when he joined her on the path.

"Forget it," he snapped, striding down the walk. What he really wanted to do was leave her to get herself back. But the child she led held him beside her. He was so frail, yet so defiantly courageous. For him and what he had already been through, he could even bear Andrea for a few more minutes.

"What the devil?" he ejaculated forcefully a second later. He halted and lifted his foot gingerly to inspect the damage done by the rock he had stepped on.

Andrea's grimace of sympathy was lost in the darkness. "Painful, aren't they?" she murmured, slowing her pace slightly.

Nick manfully held back a sarcastic dig of his own. Uncomfortable woman, he muttered silently. If there was a gentle bone in her body, he'd never seen evidence of it.

He started walking again, only to hit another rock. His oath echoed Andrea's milder epithet as she, too, stubbed her toes. He glanced up from massaging his injury to find her imitating a stork while she rubbed her foot. Her precarious balance was hampered by a silent Scrapper leaning heavily against her. She swayed awkwardly.

Without thought Nick caught her in his arms. For a second she melted against him, her head seeming to settle naturally into the hollow of his shoulder. The fresh woman scent of her surrounded him for an instant to merge with the cool dark shadows of the night. Desire, like summer lightning, shot through him, catching him unaware. He held her close, unable to release her as his mind was telling him he should.

"I'm all right now," Andrea mumbled, pushing away from him carefully. She stepped back, her gaze focused on Scrapper. To look at Nicholas was to encourage the strange lassitude invading her body. Just for a moment it had been so easy to lean on him.

"Andrea, I—" he began.

She silenced him with a gesture. "Good night, Nick, and thanks for coming this far with us." She glanced down at Scrapper. "Ready?" she asked, giving him an encouraging smile. He nodded, his eyes half closed in weariness.

Nick jammed his hands into his pockets, accepting his dismissal reluctantly. He watched her and the child walk away, feeling an inexplicable sense of loss. He had wanted to know her, to trace the shape of her with his hands. But most of all, he had wanted to taste her lips. Shrugging at the unexpected needs within him, he stood silently where she had left him. Even when the door to her cottage closed behind the two of them, he made no immediate move to return to the house. He would wait until her lights were out, he decided, just to be sure she was safe.

Moments later Andrea awkwardly tucked Scrapper into her bed and then took her place in a chair beside him. His eyes held hers as though she were the only stability in his world. Perhaps she was, she conceded, watching his lashes drift lower until he slept. Not that she made a good anchor. The little mite would have been far better off clinging to someone with more experience with children: her father, Ray or even Nick with his background in helping emotionally needy youngsters.

She rose, remembering Nick's strength, the way he caught her when she would have fallen. A man to count on in a crisis. Startled by the unexpected thought, Andrea paused briefly in the act of undressing. When had she begun to admire anything about her disapproving nemesis? she wondered.

It had been when Ray had told them about the case involving the little girl injured in that house fire where she had lost her parents, Andrea recalled almost immediately. Nick had won a hefty settlement for the child. But more importantly, he had taken a personal interest in finding her a new home with a family who loved her in spite of the scars she would always carry on her body.

Andrea settled carefully into her makeshift bed of two overstuffed chairs with an ottoman in between them for length, contemplating Nick's reaction if she told him of her admiration of his philanthropic activities. He'd probably pass out in shock, she decided, with a drowsy smile. He was too accustomed to their widely spaced sparring matches to easily believe she could find anything about him to like. On that thought, her lashes fluttered shut as sleep claimed her for the second time in one night.

Three

―――

"Do you really think you can eat all that?" Andrea asked as she placed a fourth pancake on Scrapper's plate.

He nodded, his green eyes alight with eager anticipation. Chuckling at his expression, Andrea toussled his hair before collecting her similarly laden plate. A knock at her back door interrupted them just as they were sitting down.

"You go ahead and start while I see who it is," Andrea suggested. "Nick!" The surprised exclamation escaped before she could stop it on finding him on her porch.

One dark brow lifted at her obvious shock. "Faith sent me to ask when you and Scrapper are coming up for breakfast?" he explained casually.

"Breakfast?" she echoed, casting a glance over her shoulder to the kitchen table.

Curious at her strange behavior, Nick peered around her. His eyes widened in amazement at the platter of crisp bacon, golden scrambled eggs and two plates of hotcakes. A pot of coffee shared the center of the attractive spread with a pitcher of milk.

"Where did you get the food?" he questioned blankly.

Andrea frowned, disliking the disbelief on his face much more than the occasion warranted. "I cooked it," she replied briefly. She felt the unusually good humor with which she had begun the morning dim slightly.

Nick saw the temper sparking to life in her extraordinary eyes and manfully swallowed the unwise comment he had been about to utter. "I guess you won't be coming up to the house," he substituted instead, privately wondering what he had ever done that condemned him to knowing this strange female. Her kitchen radiated a fragrantly scented welcome that was completely opposed to the tough lady image he carried in his mind.

"Want to join us?" Andrea offered, more startled than he was by her invitation. "It'll be easy enough to call Faith and tell her we're eating here."

Nick hesitated, remembering the feel of her in his arms. This was the sister of one of his best friends. He couldn't spend the rest of his life irritated by her unusual life-style nor could he continue to allow his thoughts to center on her physical appeal.

"Well?" Andrea prompted. She wished she had never opened her mouth, but she wasn't about to back out now.

"Okay," Nick decided quickly, suddenly determined to make friends with her. He would forget what she did and try to view her objectively, he assured himself as he entered her home for the first time.

"How many pancakes do you want?" she asked as she gestured for him to take a seat.

"Three should do it," he answered, following her to the stove. "Tell me where you keep the silverware and I'll set a place."

Andrea looked at him quickly, starting to make one of the usual snappy returns she seemed to reserve just for him, then caught herself. Something in his expression held her silent. Was that a plea for a truce she saw there? She stared into his eyes for a moment, aware as never before of the sheer masculine allure he exuded. "In the drawer behind you," she murmured, forcibly dragging her wayward senses in line.

She turned back to the stove, using the mundane task of cooking to restore a measure of normality to the morning. What imp had prompted her to commit herself to sharing a meal with this man? She wondered how quickly she could feed him and get him out of her house. Hopefully, she'd manage that feat before either of them started anything in front of Scrapper. Determined to be on her best behavior, Andrea collected Nick's plate to carry it to the table.

The sight of Scrapper industriously working his way through his breakfast brought a pleased curve to her lips as she took her seat. She glanced away, somehow snagging Nick's eyes. In them she saw reflected the same pleasure she was feeling.

A smile quivered on her lips, the first natural one she'd ever given him.

For a second he held her gaze, his own curiously intent. An impulse he made no attempt to stifle made him return her smile with one of his own.

"Hello, Andrea. I'm Nick." He extended his hand across the table, waiting tensely for her response. Would she accept this as a new beginning?

Andrea studied his aquamarine eyes, looking for some elusive element she sensed building between them. "Why?"

His lips tilted upwards at her blunt question. "I think it's time we buried the hatchet somewhere else besides in each other," he replied honestly.

Caught off guard by his humor, Andrea looked at him blankly for a moment. As his words sank in, she smiled and put her hand in his. "It'll be safer anyway," she added when his fingers encircled hers in a warm clasp.

"Infinitely," he agreed, releasing her reluctantly. "Now, pretty lady, let's eat before this gets cold."

Andrea picked up her fork, conscious of a sudden lightness enveloping her. The fatigue and dissatisfaction that had plagued her for the last few weeks were strangely absent. The fragrantly scented kitchen and the man and the boy sharing her table were somehow unexpectedly right.

"You know, I believe that's the first compliment you've ever given me," she mused aloud.

Nick grinned companionably. "Would you like another?" he asked in a pseudoserious tone.

"Yes." She laughed softly, enjoying his teasing in spite of being amazed at this unexpected facet of his personality.

"You're a good cook."

A vigorous nod accompanied by the faintest of smiles from Scrapper drew their attention and set the mood for the morning. Their new accord lasted through breakfast, spilling out into the sunshine as the three of them went up to the main house to clean out Andrea's rig.

"Scrapper needs cleaning up almost as much as my tractor," Andrea observed, her gaze following the boy as he tentatively played with her older nephew. "In spite of that bath last night, he looks dirty."

Nick leaned against the bumper of the cab, his long, denim-clad legs crossed at the ankles in front of him. "What he needs are some new clothes."

Andrea frowned, once more faced with her own inadequacies. Why hadn't she thought of that herself? "I could ask Faith to go with us," she murmured, knowing she would do better with some help.

"Why not me?" Nick suggested easily. "I was a little boy myself once. I think I might be able to remember what I wore."

He glanced at her, liking the way she tipped her head while she considered his offer. She seemed so much softer, more gentle than he would've expected.

Her awkwardness while she tried to deal with the needs of one small child was oddly endearing. She was obviously out of her depth, yet she still managed to handle Scrapper far better than the rest of them. Her tenderness, combined with a no-nonsense approach, was uniquely her own.

"All right," she decided finally. "Scrapper takes to you more than he does to my family, so it probably would be best." Not for anything would she admit how much she had enjoyed his company.

Nick schooled his expression not to reveal the slight disappointment he felt in her answer. "Do we go now?" he asked instead.

"I have to return the rig to the yard so I can pick up my car," she explained, suddenly wondering what to do about Scrapper. He had made a point of keeping her in sight since he had awakened. It was impossible to believe he would allow her to leave him with Nick while she took care of business.

"That sounds simple enough." Nick pushed away from his resting spot and gestured for Scrapper to join them. "We'll ride with you. It'll give our friend another chance to ride with the Purple Flash."

"How did you—You can't—" Andrea muttered. Her amethyst eyes widened before she took a breath and began again. "Riders aren't usually allowed in the trucks. Last night was a special case."

Ignoring the first part of her disjointed comment, Nick focused on the second. "We can because Big Jack owns the company, remember?" He bent to scoop up Scrapper in his arms. Two pairs of eyes stared at her expectantly. "Coming, Flash?" he drawled her nickname, imitating the truckers' down-south twang perfectly.

"I'm going to wring Ray's neck the minute I see him again," she threatened half-seriously as she opened the passenger door. "I thought lawyers were supposed to be more closemouthed."

Nick boosted Scrapper onto the seat before leaning toward Andrea until his lips grazed her ear. "Shall I tell you what other things Ray's told me about you over the years?"

Andrea stepped back, shaking her head distract-edly. "No," she got out quickly. "We have a truce, remember?"

She moved away, glad to put some distance be-tween them before he could answer. She didn't want to discuss her much-disputed life-style with him, especially now when she was feeling so edgy and rest-less about it herself. She mounted up, slammed the door shut, then checked to be sure Scrapper was set.

"Ready?" she asked with a deliberate smile, deter-mined to recapture her relaxed mood. The boy nod-ded eagerly, his eyes running swiftly over the fascinating array of dials and gauges that had in-trigued him so much the night before.

Avoiding Nick's silent stare, she started the engine as Scrapper pointed to the CB. Correctly interpreting his questioning look, Andrea's lips curved into a more natural smile. "Yes, you can turn it on," she agreed while easing the eighteen-wheeler out of the drive onto the street.

"You handle that like a pro."

Startled at Nick's quiet compliment, Andrea swung her head, a ready comment on her lips. Expecting to find him teasing if not mocking her, she discovered instead that he was talking to Scrapper. For a second, she allowed her gaze to linger on him as he unobtrusively steadied the curious child.

Some truce, she berated herself on realizing how prepared she was to jump to her own defense. Vowing to change her attitude, she concentrated on finding a neutral topic of conversation.

"You never did say how you ended up spending the night at Pop's," she began.

Nick's eyes lifted to her face, sparkling with amusement at her less than tactful comment. "Actually you can thank the courts and the Cochran case for my arrival. The verdict came through on Friday. Since I was so close I decided to drop in on Ray and Faith. I had no idea they, in turn, were staying at your father's while the decorator took over their place." He shrugged slightly. "By the time I realized where I would be sleeping, Faith, with Big Jack's approval, had invited me to stay the weekend."

"That sounds like Pop. He always has preferred the house filled with people. I think we were probably the only family on the block that gave triple parties. A barbecue in the back for Ray and his older crowd, Ned's group playing pool in the basement and mine blowing the walls down with the stereo."

"Did you have boys at your bashes?" he asked, giving no thought to how his words sounded.

For once Andrea accepted his remark at face value. His open curiosity allowed no misunderstanding. "Naturally. Half the time, because of my brothers, I had more boys than girls," she added. "I enjoyed those years, even school wasn't as bad as it could have been."

"You sound like you didn't really want to go. Is that why you didn't attend college?" he hazarded, finally exploring the area that had always bothered him. Both Ray and Ned had gone on with their education, Ray in law and Ned in business administration. But Andrea had hit the road almost the moment she had graduated.

"In a way," she admitted, thinking back on that difficult long ago decision. "I hated being closeted in one place all day. I wanted to see all the things I read about. I wanted to touch the Empire State Building, not just study a picture, swim in the Pacific instead of wondering if it was as warm as the Atlantic. I've seen golden fields of wheat, the muddy Mississippi, cherry orchards and orange groves rich with the sweet smell of citrus blossoms. I've watched the sun set in a blaze of color across a barren desert and I've watched the moon shine its silver light over snow-covered mountains." Memories of long, lonely miles stretching over dark ribbons of highways disappeared under the bounty of all she had experienced. "I've been from sea to shining sea and everywhere I've gone there has been beauty, some subtle, some obvious, but always there." She glanced at him, a little shocked at what she'd revealed.

Nick felt as though he were seeing her clearly for the first time. "I've really misjudged you all along, haven't I?" he murmured, his voice deepening with his discovery.

Andrea held his gaze for a second before returning her attention to the road. "I never set out to prove myself in a man's world. With Pop owning a trucking company, trucks just happened to be all I knew and they also were my ticket to see this land we call ours." Her shoulders lifted in a gesture of dismissal. "I used the tools I had to accomplish what I wanted out of life."

"Wanted?" he repeated, catching an elusive hint of something in her voice he didn't understand.

Ignoring his careful probing for the moment, Andrea guided her rig through the high, chain link fence that surrounded the yard of Carpenter Trucking. Why had she betrayed her nebulous feelings to him, of all people? How could she expect that he would even begin to comprehend the vague emptiness, the need for something more than the life of perpetual wanderer?

"Andrea?" Nick prompted quietly the moment she cut the engine of the big semi.

Andrea turned to him, forgetting the child who listened without seeming to and the hive of activity going on around them. "Leave it, Nick," she half commanded, half pleaded. "Put it down to a series of long cross-countries and a string of too many motel rooms.

Nick reached out to catch the hand lying motionless on her right knee. The shadows of uncertainty in her eyes, which he had always remembered as vibrantly alive, worried him more than he would have believed possible.

"I don't buy that. But I'll accept that I have no right to seek your confidence." He hesitated, sensing with his well-developed instincts that she was approaching some kind of crossroads in her life. He wanted to help her, but how could he, given his earlier attitude? "If you want to talk, I'd like to listen," he offered finally.

Andrea glanced down at their clasped hands, conscious of the warmth and strength in his grasp. Two days ago, if anyone had asked, she'd have said she disliked Nick intensely. He was narrow-minded, biased and altogether too quick to judge where she was concerned.

But today she was discovering that perhaps she had been as wrong about him as he was about her. He was perceptive, picking up her discontent with an ease that amazed her. He had demonstrated an unexpected sensitivity when she had withdrawn from him. He had neither mocked her feelings nor demanded her confidence.

Her eyes softened to the gentle purple of rainwashed violets. "Thanks," she whispered simply before carefully removing her fingers from his hold.

"You'll remember what I said?" he asked, needing the reassurance of knowing she realized he meant his offer, that it was more than just empty words without meaning or substance.

"I won't forget," she promised before focusing on the child who sat patiently waiting between them.

"How would you like to see a whole bunch of trucks?" she questioned in an altered tone. Green eyes lit up with anticipation, mutely answering her. "I'm going to introduce you and Nick to our head mechanic, Jimmy, for a grand tour while I stop by dispatch for my Monday run. Can I count on you to behave?"

Scrapper tipped his head, considering her suggestion with obvious doubt. He gazed out the tractor window, pointing to a tall lanky man heading in their direction.

Andrea shook her head, easily deciphering his basic sign language. "No, not him." She put a hand on his shoulder, urging him to look farther to the left. "See the gray-haired guy working on that motor? That's Jimmy. He used to watch me when I was about your age. In fact, he taught me how to repair these babies." She touched the steering wheel lightly. "Of course, that was a reward for minding my manners."

She waited while Scrapper thought her words over. Finally, he nodded before thrusting his hand into Nick's. He looked at her for approval. "Right." She opened her door and got out to walk to the front of the rig.

"You've got bribery down to a fine art," Nick murmured, his expression conveying his admiration of her handling of the situation.

"When you're as much of a novice at this as I am, any port looks good in a storm," she whispered back. His smile at her reply did strange things to her equilibrium. The yard faded into insignificance. The morning sun bathed them in gold, turning his blue-green eyes into sunlit seas. She inhaled the warm male scent of him, liking the way his height fit hers. His body contours were a masculine match to her own softer curves. Whispers of awareness feathered over her. The delicate sensory touching was shattered by a cheerful male voice.

"Hey, Andy, whatcha doin' down here at this hour?"

Andrea stepped back a pace, forcing herself to focus on Jimmy's wizened face. "I brought the rig in and—" she laid her hand on Scrapper's shoulder "—I brought a very special friend of mine to see you. He's truck mad." She smiled at the child as she introduced them. "Nick here, will go along with you," she added, silently indicating the child's lack of speech when Scrapper was occupied eyeing the various transports in the busy area. Other than a raised eyebrow and a sharp glance at the youngster, Jimmy took the news without comment.

"I'll stop by the shop when I'm done," she explained to Scrapper before taking her leave.

She raised her eyes from her small friend to find Nick studying her intently. For an instant she froze, reading the searching quality of his gaze with curiosity. What was he looking for? she wondered as she turned away. He was acting as if he had never seen her before, as if she were a stranger he had just met. She shrugged aside her odd impressions, unable to believe them. It had to be her unusual mood that was creating these illusions.

She headed for the large building housing her father's office, the dispatcher and the main terminal. Several men paused briefly at their jobs to greet her as she passed. Saturday was a work day just like any other at Carpenter's. The goods had to roll, so men had to load and unload regardless of weather or the hours that governed most other careers. Here a day could easily be much longer than the usual eight hours. A multitude of products crossed the docks every week destined for cities both near and far. It was the drivers and these men here whose responsibility it was to see the cargoes safely from seller to buyer.

Andrea entered the dispatch office to find Ned working at his desk, a familiar frown of concentration wrinkling his forehead. For a moment he was unaware of her presence. She knew Ned enjoyed his work as a dispatcher. It had been his choice almost from the second he graduated from college and he was good at it. He was responsible for matching drivers with loads as well as keeping communications open between the trucks and the office. When a man had trouble on the route, Ned took care of it, either by wiring money, telling the driver how to get help or sending one of Jimmy's work crews out to handle the problem. He made an indispensable contribution to Carpenter's. On the day Big Jack retired, Ned would take his place as head of the family business, but until then she, Ned and Big Jack were a team.

"Hi'ya, Andy," Ned rumbled, glancing up to find her in the doorway. "How's the boy?" He waved her to the chair in front of his desk.

"Right now he's dogging Jimmy's footsteps," she replied with a grin, taking her seat. She dropped the papers for the load she had brought in before him. "Sorry about last night."

Ned grinned, his expression unconsciously mirroring that of his father's the night before. "Forget it. If it hadn't been for the fact that the little devil was scared, I would've half laughed myself to death. That boy of yours had everyone of us buffaloed." He held up a hand to display a small set of teeth marks. "He moves like greased lightning when he wants to. He was down those stairs before we could catch him. He even had sense enough to scoot behind that chair in the corner where nobody could get him." He chuckled, his eyes twinkling. "I had half expected him to throw those things off that knickknack shelf, but he didn't until the boys started egging him on." He paused in his recounting to look at her. "What are you going to do with him when you go out again?" He reached for his roster. "You've got a trip Monday."

"So?" Andrea shrugged. "Ray's sure to have something on his parents by then. He notified the police last night, you know."

"But what if he doesn't? Do you want me to give your ticket to another driver?" He shook his head over his own stupidity. "I take that back. When have you ever refused a load." It was a statement, not a question.

"I think this time I'd better make an exception."

"What?" Ned's astonishment was plain. "I don't believe it." He studied her silently for a moment.

Andrea met his gaze, knowing what he would see, what he had always seen: stubbornness. A slender face marked by clearly molded cheekbones and well-defined features. Her slightly square chin, a legacy from her father, hinted at her attitude. In her family's more humorous moments, she was known as the wandering gypsy, thanks to her gleaming black hair and deep violet eyes.

"What gives?" Ned asked quietly, his concern evident in his voice. "You look tired."

"I am," she admitted with a sigh. "To my bones." She gazed at a point beyond him, suddenly needing to confide in him. Ned had always been the closer of her two brothers. "I've been thinking about cutting down on the long hauls." She dropped her idea in his lap to await his reaction. It was quick in coming.

"What's really wrong? You used to thrive on traveling. You've handled a far rougher schedule than you've had for the past couple of months without any trouble."

"I'm almost thirty," she pointed out, indirectly answering him. "I'm beginning to wonder if I'm just playing around with my life. I've seen all I wanted to see, but what have I really done?" She refocused on her brother, her expression gravely questioning.

The understanding in Ned's eyes warmed her. "Have you talked to Pop?" he asked gently.

She shook her head, knowing her reply surprised him. She and her father had always been close, soul mates in a way no one else in the family was with her. Big Jack had roamed in his youth just as she was doing until one day he had met Catherine, her mother, and married her.

"There hasn't been time yet," she explained slowly.

Ned frowned, his gaze direct but troubled. "Would you like to take a vacation? You haven't had one, a real one, I mean, in a couple of years."

Andrea considered his suggestion carefully. Perhaps that was the answer. Maybe she just needed a rest. "Can you spare me?" There was no conceit in her question, only a simple statement of fact.

Ned inclined his dark head. "No problem. I can easily give you three weeks."

Startled at the block of time he'd offered her, she stared at him in silence. Would twenty-one days ease the dissatisfaction plaguing her and return her life to its usual even tenor?

"I'll take it," she decided finally, having no other real choice. She wanted her life back in order as soon as possible.

Four

Andrea stared at her reflection in amazement. Was that really her? she wondered, surprised at the image before her. Nick had been right when he had urged her to buy this dress. The delicate lavender lace was far removed from her usual style. The sleek sophistication of the strapless top and figure hugging lines accentuated her slender curves to perfection. She had never looked so attractive in her life.

"Or felt so strange," she murmured aloud. She half whirled, frowning slightly at the sexy image she projected. She hadn't realized her legs were so long and slender, nor her breasts so full. The light from the vanity lamp caught the amethyst studs in her ears, adding flashes of deep purple. Maybe she'd been a little heavy with the makeup. She studied her face carefully, then shook her head. No, if anything the cosmetics she had used, especially the shaded lavender eye colors, were more understated than what most women wore.

The knock at the door interrupted her self-examination. Taking a deep breath, Andrea sought to calm the sudden flutter in her midsection. It was only an evening out with Faith and Ray. And Nick, a little voice whispered, refusing to allow her to forget his presence.

"I'm ready," she offered, the moment she opened the door. She smiled, pretending a casualness she was far from feeling.

Nick's eyes widened at the sight of her, his gaze making a slow appreciative sweep. She was beautiful, he realized in astonishment as he focused on her face. Deep purple eyes stared back at him, holding a surprising degree of uncertainty. Uncertainty? Andrea?

"You're lovely." Prompted by an impulse, he stepped forward to brush his lips over hers. It was a light caress meant to reassure her. Yet from the first touch, Nick was aware of something different. Somehow she drew him to deepen the kiss. His arms encircled her as his mouth settled on hers, obeying the unspoken command.

Unprepared for Nick's greeting, Andrea was slow in reacting. Before she knew what was happening, her lips had softened before his gentle invasion, granting him access to her mouth. His arms cradled her against him, making her aware of him with every particle of her being. His silk shirt brushed against her bare shoulders, sending whispers of sensation over her skin. His spicy after-shave teased her with a fragrant invitation to move closer. His warmth enfolded her as she relaxed against him for a fleeting instant.

Then she stiffened, suddenly conscious of the seductive danger of this man. She drew her arms down to wedge them between their bodies as she edged back. She saw the embers of desire he made no effort to hide.

"I won't let you do this," she breathed, releasing her unguarded words in a rush. "I'm not one of your crowd. I've never learned how to play games with my emotions."

Nick's brows drew together in a frown at her stark comment. "What crowd?" he demanded, going from wanting her to needing an explanation in an instant. He released her abruptly. Was this odd female accusing him of being a womanizer? The idea irritated him to the point of anger. He was no saint, but he was no seducer, either.

"You know what I mean," she returned, striving for composure. She was out of her depth and she knew it. "Look at me." She waved a hand at her fashionable new self.

Nick studied her silently. It took him a moment to figure out it wasn't his life-style bothering her, but her own. With that knowledge his temper died to be replaced by a softer, more understanding mood. "I'm looking but all I see is what got me into trouble," he drawled, his lips twitching at the faint belligerence in her expression.

"Don't you dare laugh at me. I'm serious," she warned, her doubts surfacing. "All day you've been so nice, I've felt like I was shopping with a stranger. You were patient with Scrapper through all the trying on he did. Lunch was fun. You even managed to bully me, in the gentlest way, of course, into buying this dress."

"So?" In spite of his best efforts, he could feel a grin forming.

Andrea tried to ignore his humor but without success. A smile tugged at her lips, holding more than a little self-directed amusement. "You're staring at probably one of Massachusetts' oldest late bloomers. I can't even remember the last time I had on a skirt," she added in case he had missed the point.

"Andrea Carpenter," he teased, his expression conveying his understanding, "I think I like you, late blooming and all, just the way you are." He lifted his hands to cradle her face in his palms. "My crowd, as you call it, knows a lot about sophisticated tricks, witty conversation and current events. But none of them could have matched your description of your traveling, no woman I know would have succeeded so well with Scrapper and I guarantee you not one of them could grace that dress more beautifully than you do."

Andrea searched his sea-colored eyes to find only sincerity in the aquamarine depths. Relief and a strange sense of rightness filled her. One by one her doubts fled. "Why is it I believe you?" she asked, scarcely aware that she spoke aloud.

"Because it's true. And despite your self-professed inexperience, you know it." He gently caressed her throat with his thumbs. "I'll promise you something if you like. I won't treat you like someone you're not. I'll always remember who and what you are."

Puzzled at his reassurance, Andrea frowned. "I don't understand."

Nick released her slowly, his hands drifting to her shoulders. "You don't have to, right now." He smiled disarmingly, his eyes crinkling at the corners. "We'd better go. Ray and Faith are waiting for us at the house."

He let her go to collect the matching wrap lying on the table to his left. In one smooth motion, he draped it around her shoulders before handing her the handbag. In seconds, Andrea found her arm tucked in his, her door locked and herself escorted down the path as though she was a delicate creature of infinite value. Neither spoke as they walked the short distance to the main house.

"I love your dress," Faith exclaimed excitedly the instant they all settled in Nick's car. She edged forward on the back seat, her dark brown eyes nearly black in the dim interior. "Wherever did you find it? It's a fantastic color, almost hyacinth."

"At that new mall. There's a little boutique by the east entrance," Andrea replied easily. Faith's outgoing personality was infectious, making a lively discussion out of an ordinary one. "I spotted it while I was waiting for Nick and Scrapper."

"I saw the pajamas you bought the boy. He's so proud of his new clothes, you'd think he'd won the lottery."

"I wish he had," Ray commented gravely.

Andrea stiffened at the sudden intrusion of seriousness. But before she could question her brother's meaning, Nick spoke.

"Have you heard something?" he asked, flicking Andrea a quick glance.

"The only child reported missing so far doesn't fit Scrapper's description. Nor does it mention he's a mute."

"Don't say that," Andrea snapped, shocking herself with her swift refusal to accept anyone labeling Scrapper. "He may not communicate like you or I, but he's far from speechless."

Nick caught her hand, giving it a gentle squeeze. "He didn't mean it like that," he soothed her quietly for the second time that day. The first incident like this one had amazed him. Her protectiveness had been as fierce as it was unexpected. She had almost torn a strip off a clothes salesman who had dared to suggest that Scrapper wasn't cooperating with him.

Andrea grimaced at her own reaction. Of course Ray hadn't been intentionally derogatory. He was simply stating a fact. "Sorry, Ray," she murmured, giving him an apologetic look.

He inclined his head before continuing. "It's possible he could have hitched a ride to the rest stop somehow, but neither I nor the police think so."

"I tried questioning him again about where he came from, but I still didn't have any luck," Andrea admitted. Unconsciously she tightened her grip on Nick's hand. "What do you think will happen to him if we don't find his people?"

Nick returned the pressure of her fingers, hearing the anxiety and concern behind her query. "Then I'll see about getting him sent to Seven Oaks. Our people there are especially good with children and their problems."

"Seven Oaks?" Andrea repeated, knowing the name was familiar, yet unable to recall its significance.

"Good Lord, Andy, don't you remember me telling you about the home Nick endowed?" Ray questioned from the back seat.

"Ray." Nick's warning for silence was unmistakable.

"Go on," Andrea directed, glancing at Nick's controlled profile. "What is Seven Oaks?"

"It's simply a tax write-off," Nick explained before Ray could reply. "My family's estate was too large and too expensive to keep up for just me so I and some friends of mine set up a fund to run it as a kind of emergency home and halfway house for youngsters in need."

"What he means is for children who aren't adoptable for one reason or another," Faith put in, admiration evident in her voice. "Ray and I visited it last summer. It's really a special place and nothing at all like most of the facilities allotted to children. There's a real family feeling. Scrapper could be happy there."

Andrea gazed straight ahead as Faith's reassurance poured over her. She had great respect for her petite sister-in-law. She was not only good with her sons and Ray but also with the various children they had taken in over the years. So why was she rejecting the idea of sending Scrapper away? She should be relieved, she reminded herself. She had never wanted or meant for him to be a part of her life. Yet in twenty-four short hours he had become just that. He had elbowed and kicked his way into her heart without her being aware of it.

"Andrea?"

Nick's smooth voice curled around her, pulling her out of her musings. "He doesn't have to come to us," he began carefully.

Andrea shook her head, forcing a faint smile to her lips. "I was just thinking, not objecting," she denied, suddenly wondering what any of them would say if she suggested keeping Scrapper. She could imagine Ray and Faith's shock, and until recently, Nick's. But now she had a feeling he would be far less startled than her family.

Nick flicked her a swift probing look before easing his car into the restaurant's almost full parking lot. Something was bothering her. He could feel it, but he didn't understand it. Given her life-style, he would have thought the responsibility of a child would be the last thing she would have chosen for herself, even on the present, temporary basis.

Faith, with Ray at her side, joined them. "Nick, quit frowning," Faith commanded gaily, apparently unaware of the undercurrents.

Clearing his expression, he took Andrea's arm. "Like Andrea, I was thinking," he returned blandly.

"Tomorrow you can do all of that you like, but tonight we're going to enjoy ourselves. Andrea needs a break from traveling, you and Ray from your dusty tomes, and dry as dust presentations, and I from a long week of paint swatches, wallpaper books and fabric samples." She linked arms with her husband to smile mischievously up at him. "And no shoptalk, you promised," she reminded him.

Ray laughed at his wife's decree. "Is she trying to tell us something?" He quirked a dark brow at Nick and Andrea.

"At a guess, I'd say so," Andrea drawled, privately more than happy to comply with Faith's wishes.

They entered the tastefully appointed foyer to find themselves in a small crowd of would-be diners. Nick released Andrea to stroll forward to confer with the formally attired hostess poised at the doorway of the main dining room. A moment later the four of them were following the slender blonde to a reserved table overlooking a garden setting.

"I swear half the reason I like to eat here is because of the atmosphere," Faith confided as Ray seated her.

Andrea nodded, smiling at her brown-haired sister by marriage. "It is beautiful," she agreed, her gaze roaming appreciatively over the wine-and-gold decor. The subdued murmur of conversation barely impinged on the elegant intimacy of the widely spaced tables. This was one of Springfield's most popular dining spots where, because of the limited seating, reservations were essential.

"Ladies, what will you have?" Nick asked, dividing his glance between the two women.

"White wine?" Andrea turned to check with Faith.

"Suits me," she agreed. She waited until their waiter departed before she spoke again. "Now what nonsense shall we discuss? Anyone have any ideas?"

Silence. Andrea looked at Nick to find him watching her. "Talk about how to dry up four tongues," she observed.

He grinned, shrugging slightly. "I think we've all just gotten a lesson in how boxed in we are in our own concerns," he countered drolly. "We could argue current events."

"Or how to repair a truck engine," Andrea shot back quickly, remembering the earlier conversation about his crowd versus her experience.

The flash of amusement in his eyes at her sally brought a chuckle bubbling forth. He had understood her reference immediately.

"How about the story of my overflowing washer and the missing repairman?" Faith inserted, joining the game.

"I like the one about the flasher who got out on bail in time to finalize the purchase of his new business, a men's clothing store," Ray suggested, his usually serious face creasing into a grin that sparked outright laughter in his listeners.

With that the tone was set for the evening. Wine, perfectly prepared food and good company created a lighthearted atmosphere that was relaxing and stimulating at one and the same time.

Andrea saw Nick in a new guise. He was an excellent host, always aware of her and his guests' wishes. Yet he showed himself far more human than she would ever have suspected. His wit, while not of the obviously funny type like Faith's, was dry with a faint sting. The blend was provocative as well as amusing. Andrea had never enjoyed herself more.

By the time they entered the club Faith had suggested for dancing, Andrea had decided her long-held opinion of Nick was totally useless.

"Shall we try our luck, Andrea?"

Andrea glanced up to see Nick leaning over her. She turned her head slightly to survey the comfortably filled dance floor. "I'm not very good," she explained carefully.

Nick caught her hand to urge her to her feet. "My shoes will survive," he replied easily, leading her through the tables. He swung her into his arms in perfect time to the languid beat. "I've been waiting to hold you all evening."

Andrea stiffened slightly, in the process missing a step. "Don't," she whispered before she could stop herself. She had been enjoying his company too much to want to remember how his kiss had affected her.

Nick pulled her gently against him, ignoring her resistance. "Relax, I'm not going to pounce on you. Not now, not ever."

Hearing the undeniable sincerity in his voice, Andrea found her body instinctively obeying his soft command. Tension flowed out of her as she let his subtle guidance and the music take over. He held her close enough to feel his every movement, yet there was no unnerving sexuality in his embrace. Instead, she knew a sense of well-being mixed with pleasure, a curious feeling of homecoming.

One mellow tune merged into another, weighting her limbs with a delicious languor. She sighed softly as her head dropped to nestle in the curve of his throat. "I never knew dancing was so nice," she mumbled.

Nick tightened his arms fractionally before reminding himself to curb his interest. She had warned him once that she was inexperienced. He eased his grip slightly before tucking her hand against his chest. "Are you enjoying yourself?" he asked huskily.

He inhaled deeply, breathing in her scent with unexpected greed. The touch of her body against his was bringing alive a need that was stronger than any he had ever experienced. Andrea was fast becoming an intriguing, complex creature whom he desired. Andy, the female truck driver, was a fading memory. And, for the first time in his life, he was unsure how to proceed. Yet he couldn't stop seeing her, he realized suddenly.

"Do you think we should call it a night soon?" Andrea asked. She was too content to really want to leave, but she was conscious of Scrapper sleeping at her father's house. "Pop's a great sitter, but Scrapper might have another nightmare." When the music drifted to an end, she lifted her head from its resting place. She stared into the blue-green eyes so close to her own. For a second neither spoke while all around them couples were leaving the floor.

"Don't get too attached to Scrapper," Nick cautioned gravely. Where before he would've never thought her to be vulnerable enough to need his warning, now he knew better. "It will only hurt you more when you let him go." A muscle twitched in his cheek revealing his restraint on a more forcibly given suggestion. Concern and understanding etched his features as he held her gaze.

"I'm already attached," she admitted honestly.

"Damn," Nick muttered in an uncharacteristic oath. He caught her hands in his warm grasp. "He can't stay with you, you know that."

She nodded. "I've never once thought he could." She blinked, feeling emotions she had never known well up within her. She had the strangest urge to lean her head on his shoulder and let him hold her.

"Come on, honey, let's get out of here." Nick slipped an arm around her waist.

At another earlier time, she would have shaken off such a gesture from Nick. But at this moment, she welcomed his unspoken support. Nor had he made any comment about her undoubted foolishness in be-

coming so closely involved with Scrapper. She knew
as well as he did what an unlikely parent she was. And
it wasn't her single state that was the stumbling block.
It was her nomadic way of life.

All these thoughts and more occupied her mind on
the nearly silent drive back to Big Jack's. In the back
seat, Faith leaned her head against Ray's shoulder in
drowsy relaxation, leaving most of the talking to the
men. The downstairs lights of the main house glowed
as Nick pulled to a halt in the driveway.

"I wonder what's up?" Andrea sat upright, curiosity driving away her introspective mood. "I hope
Scrapper isn't at it again," she added as she got out of
the car. Ray and Faith were right behind them, though
neither exhibited the same concern Andrea did.

"If he is, your father will cope," Nick assured her
while matching her swift stride up the walk. "Your
foundling wasn't nearly as clingy when we left as he
had been. And Jack was obviously happy to have three
boys instead of two to enjoy."

Andrea opened the door just as her father entered
the hall from the living room. "What happened?" she
demanded without preamble on seeing the worry lining his broad features.

"I'm glad you're home," he replied, shaking his
dark gray head wearily. In that moment he looked
every one of his fifty-eight years. "The police rang
about an hour ago. They've located Scrapper's people." His eyes held a deep well of compassion for his
youngest offspring.

Andrea stared at him, barely aware of Nick sliding an arm about her shoulders. "They're sure?"

He nodded. "The missing child could not speak," he added gently.

Five

"Let's go into the living room where we can all get comfortable," Nick suggested, urging Andrea forward.

Andrea made no effort to resist the gentle pressure he exerted. She was incapable of doing anything at that moment. They were going to take Scrapper away from her.

"Who lost him and why?" she demanded as Nick sat down with her beside him. She fixed her father with a probing look.

"His aunt and uncle." Big Jack settled his muscular frame into his favorite armchair. "Scrapper's name is really Danny Winters. His parents were killed in an auto accident a couple of weeks ago outside of Williamsburg, Virginia. The aunt, the mother's sister, and her husband live in Boston. They went down for the funeral and to pick up Scrapper. They were on their way home when Scrapper slipped away from them at the rest stop where you found him."

Anger was the first emotion Andrea was conscious of. How could two adults possibly lose one child? "Why wasn't he reported missing sooner?"

"He was." He glanced briefly at his older son. "That description you were given earlier was Danny. In their shock over losing the boy his relatives forgot all about his speech problem."

"Forgot!" Andrea echoed incredulously. "How the devil could they have forgotten something as important as that?"

"Andrea," Nick soothed, sensing her chaotic feelings through the rigid tension holding her motionless and unnaturally erect beside him. "People do strange things in a crisis."

"They already had five children of their own with them," Big Jack explained, watching his usually sunny-tempered daughter closely. "It was late and they'd been on the road all day. According to the police, they were pushing to get home."

"Dragging six kids along without a thought," she exclaimed angrily, knowing how tiring and boring such a trip would be for anyone, let alone for children. The more she heard, the less she liked his aunt and uncle. They hardly sounded like fit guardians for a child such as Scrapper.

"When are they coming to get him?" Nick asked, almost hating to voice the question in front of Andrea.

Jack gave him a grateful look. "Tomorrow before noon."

Nick nodded before glancing significantly toward the door.

Jack rose and crossed to Andrea. He touched her cheek with a hand scored with calluses. "I know how much you care about the little mite, but don't tear yourself up like this," he ordered in a deep rumble.

Andrea looked up at him, her lips curving into a faint self-mocking smile. "First Nick, now you," she murmured. "I can't change what's already happened."

He inclined his head, accepting her words without surprise. Her concern and caring had been apparent to all of them from the first. "Why don't you leave the boy here tonight? He needs his sleep and you need to calm down. He's had enough emotional upsets. He may notice your mood and that's going to make tomorrow all the harder for him."

"Okay, Pop." She knew his advice made sense. Suddenly she was conscious of Faith and Ray's silent but sympathetic presence. Comforted by her family's support, she watched them quietly file out.

She turned to find Nick watching her, compassion deepening his sea-tinted eyes. "I'm all right," she whispered hoarsely.

He ignored the blatant untruth. "I know you're worried, Andrea. I know, too, you didn't like the sounds of the aunt and her family. I didn't, either, but both of us could be jumping to conclusions.''

She searched his expression, wondering why she felt better because he agreed with her. "Can we do anything to protect him?"

"Nowadays children have far more rights and people to look after them than they've ever had. We'll watch over Scrapper some way even if it means legally removing him to Seven Oaks." He hesitated a moment, wanting to ask something but unsure how to word his question. Finally when no tactful way presented itself, he opted for bluntness.

"Why does this child matter so much?"

Startled at the abrupt demand, Andrea was silent. How could she answer him when she had no idea herself? "I don't know," she replied honestly. "The best response I can give you is I admire his spirit. He's a fighter, a tough little guy who's meeting life, not hiding from it."

Nick lifted her hand, to cradle it in his. He stared at her slender fingers, vaguely surprised at their delicacy. "It's more than that, I think," he offered gently, carefully. He felt her tension, although she made no effort to withdraw from his grasp. "No mother on earth could have been more fiercely protective than you've been with Danny."

"Don't call him that," Andrea snapped, shocked at her own vehemence. That was their name for Scrapper, not hers.

Nick raised his head to impale her with an all too knowing scrutiny. "My God, you love that boy," he said hoarsely, the realization hitting him forcefully.

Andrea snatched her hand from his, feeling more exposed and vulnerable than she ever had in her life. "So what?" she drawled with deliberate flippancy. "He's a lovable child."

Nick's eyes widened at the unvarnished lie. "The devil he is. Except for Faith and the boys, everyone of us bears a mark or two from your 'lovable' waif," he shot back with a masculine snort of disagreement.

Andrea's brow rose as her temper flared. He was making Scrapper sound like some juvenile delinquent. "What would you have done if you had been faced with a household full of strangers after a nightmare? Probably invited everyone to tea," she suggested sarcastically. She pushed off the couch, unable to bear being near Nick. For a second she had been fooled into thinking he understood. But he didn't and, with his experience, he should. She walked angrily toward the door, only to be stopped short by a pair of hands on her shoulders. At his touch she whirled, eyes blazing, ready to let fly.

"Don't," he grated, pulling her against his chest with a groan.

"Let me go," she demanded, struggling to escape his enfolding arms. She didn't want his comfort or anything else he might offer.

Nick held her fast, absorbing her resistance with his strength. He realized he had sensed her vulnerability, even pierced her shell of self-sufficiency. And then hurt her when all he wanted to do was to help her, to support her. Fool, he berated himself silently.

"Easy, honey, I'm not your enemy," he soothed, stroking her back. "I'm just one not-so-bright male with a foot sticking up to his knee in his mouth."

Andrea gave one last futile wiggle before finally accepting that he wouldn't release her. "At least to the knee," she agreed angrily. She tried and failed to lift her head from his shoulder.

Nick's fingers gently massaged the tension corded muscles at her nape. "Trust me, Andrea. I want to help."

"Do you?" This time when she attempted to raise her head, he made no move to stop her. She searched his face to find the truth. Sincerity, concern and the determination that had made him such a good attorney were etched in every hollow and plane.

He met her eyes, seeing the wary, yet hopeful gleam in the purple depths. "Yes." He waited, wondering if she would trust him even a little. He had made so many wrong assumptions in the past, he was almost afraid to blink. He needed her to believe him, he realized, more than he would have thought possible. The relief that coursed through him when she relaxed against him was as heady as the finest vintage.

"You won't regret it," he assured her swiftly, huskily. He dropped his arms, carefully concealing his desire to bury himself for a moment in her softness. This time he would make no mistakes. He had learned his lesson. Andrea was a law unto herself and he wanted her. And he was going to do his best to make her want him with the same urgency that fired his blood.

"It's late," Andrea murmured, feeling strangely reluctant to leave.

He inclined his head, stepping away to allow her to precede him into the hall. "I'll walk you back."

The night air was cool on her cheeks as they left the house. They strolled silently side by side down the path while a faint breeze stirred the leaves on the trees in a gentle melody. Andrea was past thinking. The worry over Scrapper, her own unease about the future and the strange affinity she was beginning to recognize she had for Nick were a chaotic jumble in her mind. She had no clear answers or explanations for any of it. She mounted the steps to her porch.

"Invite me in," he commanded deeply, without touching her.

She shook her head in an unconscious gesture of refusal. "Not tonight. I can't think straight right now."

"What else is bothering you?" He watched her intently. He could see the confusion, the uncertainty in her eyes. "Can I help?"

Andrea's lips curved into a slight smile at the irony of his offer. "You could, but I don't know if you will."

He lifted a brow at her cryptic reply. "Explain, please." He took a step closer.

Andrea hesitated. Should she try to put her feelings into words? Or should she simply confide her concern about her career? Briefly she wondered why she was willing to consider telling him anything.

"Andrea," he prompted, reaching out to stroke her cheek. "Talk to me."

She stared into his eyes, caught by the gentleness of his gaze. "Why are you inserting yourself into my life now?" she asked, drawn reluctantly into revealing her need to know. "We've spent years without even seeing one another. And before that neither of us had a very good opinion of the other." She raised her hands in a short arc, conveying her inadequacy at expressing the situation to date. "Why now?"

Nick caught her fingers in his, stilling her movement. "Are you asking for total honesty?" His grip tightened at her affirmative nod. "I want you," he stated starkly. "The more I get to know you, the more I want you in my arms. We're nothing alike. I know that as well as you, but that no longer seems to matter."

"An affair?" she countered, seeing some of her own doubts in his expression. "I've never had one, you know."

Nick tensed, for a moment unable to comprehend what she was saying. "You're a—" He hesitated, suddenly feeling as awkward as a teen with his first girlfriend. "How?" he closed his mouth abruptly. Stupid question. He tried again. "Why not?" He groaned, unable to believe he'd actually asked that.

Andrea's eyes widened at Nick's obvious discomfort. The smooth, polished Bostonian image was gone in a puff of smoke. The humor of their conversation struck as he came to a final stumbling halt. She chuckled, earning herself a none too pleased glare.

"Well, damn, Andrea, what do you expect, dropping a remark like that in my lap?" He let go of her hands swiftly to jam his into his pockets with a scowl. "You're twenty-eight, almost twenty-nine. When did you plan on starting?"

Andrea laughed aloud at the muted outrage in his voice. "I didn't think a woman went around planning to lose it," she replied, gasping slightly.

If anything Nick's expression grew more thunderous. "Don't be smart, you know what I mean." He stopped to stare at her piercingly. "You're not feeding me a story—" He paused, not sure if he wanted her to be untouched or not. One way, there was a possibility of a future for them. But the other— He was no taker of innocence, especially not that of his best friend's sister.

Andrea leaned against the door, unable to control her amusement. He looked and sounded horrified. She had never seen him so rattled.

Nick caught her shoulders. "Stop that, woman. This isn't funny."

Andrea peered at him through tearing eyes. "If it isn't, I don't know what is," she got out. "I thought men liked being the first."

"Not when it's with a female he's known since she was a kid with scruffy jeans," he shot back, irritably. "And not when he's as fond of said female's family as I am of yours."

"Poor Nicky," Andrea crooned, enjoying the situation more with each passing second. "Just think, after we go to bed once, it won't matter anymore."

"Damn it, don't talk like that," he all but roared. "If you haven't found someone to share yourself with, then it's because *you* haven't been affected by any man you've met." He studied her, daring her to deny his assessment.

His harshly spoken evaluation shattered Andrea's light-hearted mood. There was a beautiful compliment in his words that was unexpected. "Nick?" she questioned hesitantly.

He gazed at her, his temper dying in an instant. The soft, inky darkness of her eyes held a strangely vulnerable light. "You're an intriguing woman that any man would be proud to be with," he murmured huskily. "That's why I believed you were—" He hesitated, seeking a word to describe what he meant. But they all seemed too harsh. He didn't want her experienced or to know she'd been around, he realized with startling insight.

"Experienced?" Andrea completed his statement when he made no attempt to do so.

He shook his head, immediately rejecting the label. "Not that." He pulled her close, unable to resist the temptation. "Now what do I do with you? I can't se—" He bit off his next words with a sigh.

"You can't seduce me," Andrea mumbled, leaning against him. She lifted her head to search his face. "Were you going to try?" she asked, curiously intrigued at the possibility.

His lips twisted into an unwilling smile at her question. "It's the way the game works, you know." He kissed the tip of her nose.

She wrinkled the saluted feature saucily, wondering why she had ever sought to avoid Nick. He had a sense of humor that appealed to her and a body that was infinitely pleasing to cuddle.

"I haven't quit wanting you," he warned, suddenly serious.

Andrea recognized the question hidden in his statement. He was offering her a way out. All she had to do was tell him she wanted his friendship and nothing more. He would accept that, she knew it with a certainty that astounded her. Yet did she really want a platonic relationship? She didn't know. Part of her still preferred her old, unencumbered ways. But the new feelings she had been experiencing lately were urging her to look for more in her life. Was Nick somehow connected with the emptiness she had begun to know?

"I'm not sure what I want," she explained, deciding honesty was more important at this point. "I want to see you. I like being with you. But I don't know if I want more."

He inclined his head slowly, understanding exactly what she was saying. Relief coursed through him, alerting him to how much he had wanted her to agree to continue spending time with him. "Then we'll go on as we are." He bent his head to brush her lips lightly. For an instant he almost succumbed to the urge to steal a real taste of her. Instead he contented himself with an almost chaste caress, feeling an unusual sense of protectiveness mixed with tenderness. He released her mouth slowly, his eyes lingering on her fine-boned features. It continued to amaze him how delicately built she was for her height and her occupation. At this moment she appeared more fragile than any woman he had ever known.

"I won't be going back tomorrow until Helen Dillion comes," he said quietly, needing a reason to prolong staying with her and a diversion for his thoughts.

"I'd like that," Andrea answered simply. She sighed, realizing how much she had been depending on him being there. "Ray's good, I know—" she added, half to herself.

Nick felt a surge of pride at her confession. He hugged her against him. "I'm on your side, remember that."

She lifted her face to his. "Kiss me good-night," she commanded in a breathy whisper. Her plea was unmistakable and she knew it.

"You're playing with fire," he warned, feeling the heat build within him.

"You'll protect me from the flames," she murmured drawing his head down.

His lips touched hers, fusing them as one. It was a simple kiss, yet it affected her like the finest wine. His hands moved over her back, pulling her impossibly closer. Searing in a sensual brand, his mouth moved on hers, his tongue taking possession of the soft inner tissue in a stunning surge of hunger. Yet for all the unleashed desire, there was an underlying gentleness in the way he held her.

Andrea lost a part of herself in that moment. Her body recognized its mate with a primitive clarity. When Nick drew back, Andrea knew that knowledge lay in her eyes. She lifted her hand to his cheek, stroking the faintly rough curve with a light touch. "Have breakfast with me tomorrow?"

He smiled slightly. "And every day after that if it were possible." He released her slowly, his hands lingering over each curve as he took a step back. "I won't leave until after Scrapper's people come." He paused, studying her in the soft light. "That is if you're sure you want me to stay." Even though he knew she wanted him with her, he found he also wanted to hear her admit her need aloud again.

Andrea nodded without an instant's hesitation. Odd as it was in her self-sufficient life, she did need him and his support. "I'm glad you offered," she confessed. "I'm out of my depth in this—" She spread her fingers, indicating her feelings of inadequacy.

Nick caught her hands, squeezing them reassuringly. "Don't you believe it. None of the people working out at Seven Oaks could have done any better than you have. And they're experts."

She grimaced ruefully. "It's only been accidental," she replied uncomfortably.

"As long as it's working, it doesn't matter." He dropped her hands to cradle her face between her palms. "Smile for me so I can see the shine come back in your eyes," he commanded deeply. "No matter what happens tomorrow, I'll be with you as long as you want me."

Andrea read the grave intensity in his eyes. It matched the deep sincerity of his words. Comforted by his unreserved support, she gave him the smile he demanded. He bent his head to lightly trace the gentle curve of her lips.

"Sleep well," he whispered against her closed lashes.

Andrea opened her eyes at the evocative caress. He feathered gentle fingers over her jaw, then left. She gazed after him, slightly dazed at his abrupt departure. She touched her lips, tactilely remembering the feel of his mouth on hers.

Nick.

His name wrapped around her like a warm woolen blanket on a snowy evening. How could he make her feel so secure and so complete at this moment after all that had gone before? Where was the man who had haunted her with disapproval for so long? she wondered as she entered her cottage. What was happening to him? Better still, what was happening to her? Just for a short time she had wanted much more from Nick than a kiss or two. For an instant, she had had an almost desperate urge to have his bare skin beneath her fingers, to touch him in ways she had never thought of with another man.

"Why now?" she groaned aloud to her empty bedroom. What allure did Nick hold for her after all these years?

Six

"Will you relax," Nick commanded, catching Andrea's wrist as she started to pace past him yet again.

Andrea halted abruptly to stare at him, a worried frown marring her brow. "They should be here by now. What's keeping them?" She sprawled onto the arm of Nick's chair in response to his gentle tug on her hand.

"Traffic," he offered reasonably.

"On Sunday morning?" Her brow rose to convey her blatant skepticism. She shifted restlessly on her perch. "At least Scrapper is spared this waiting. If it's driving me nuts, it would probably be ten times worse for him."

"That's why I suggested leaving him up at the house with Ray's boys while we talked with the Dillions. Faith and Big Jack will keep them busy until we meet his people." He lightly shook her arm once, drawing her attention. "Quit fidgeting. I'll protect Scrapper for you, I promise."

Andrea nodded, knowing he was right, but unable to quell her uneasiness. "I feel so helpless," she burst out. "He's defenseless. Anything could happen to him."

Hearing the very real anguish in her voice, Nick slipped his arm around her waist. He drew her against his side, surprised to feel a tremor ripple through her. "Andrea?" Alarm and shock colored his tone as he stared at her. The shimmering liquid purple of her eyes tugged at his emotions. She looked so vulnerable, so in need of his strength.

"Stupid, isn't it, to get so worked up over one small runaway," she whispered, her words erupting unevenly in spite of her best attempts at control.

"You're tearing me apart, honey," he groaned, guiding her head to his shoulder. He wanted to wrap his arms around her and promise her anything she desired just to see a flash of spirit in her eyes. Anything was worth removing her pain. "Do you want the boy this much?" He tightened his arms about her. "It won't be easy, but we can try."

She shook her head. "I've got no experience. I'm probably no better for him than I think his aunt is." She relaxed slightly as he held her. His warmth dispelled some of the chill of the impending separation.

"I just want him happy and whole," she breathed against the sheltering hollow of his neck.

"Andrea, I—"

The noisy sound of a car pulling into her drive interrupted whatever he was going to say. Andrea stiffened, drawing away abruptly. She surged to her feet to hurry to the door. Nick was right behind her as she opened it.

"No," she whispered, her gaze held by the aged, rust-marked station wagon before her.

"Easy," Nick cautioned sympathetically while lightly touching her arm to remind her of his presence.

She inhaled a stricken gasp as a man and woman got out. Though clean and as neat as a two-hour car trip permitted, their appearance was decidedly less than reassuring.

"Mrs. Carpenter?" the man questioned hesitantly as he mounted the porch steps, his wife at his side.

"Ms Carpenter," Andrea replied automatically. "You're thinking of my sister-in-law. She's up at the house with Scrap—" she hastily corrected herself "With Danny."

"Is he really all right?" the woman questioned anxiously, her dark eyes clouded with concern. She gripped her husband's hand tightly, her gaze fixed on Andrea's face. "We've been so worried. We were sure we'd never find him." She choked back a sob.

Andrea stared at her problem-worn features, noting the swollen, red-rimmed eyes. Danny's aunt had been crying, she realized, feeling a surge of empathy for the relative she had been so prepared to dislike.

"Let's go inside," Nick suggested, summing up the situation quickly. The man nodded swiftly before urging his wife up the steps.

A moment later they were settled but ill at ease in Andrea's small living room. "Can we see Danny?"

"Helen," her husband admonished gently at her hurried spate of words. He turned to Nick. "My wife's been under a strain with the funeral and all. Danny is her sister's only child and he took his parents' passing very hard."

Nick inclined his head while giving Andrea's hand a warm squeeze. "Yet Danny ran away from you, Mr. Dillion," he pointed out expressionlessly.

"Call me Burt, not that Mr. Dillion stuff." He met Nick's eyes without hesitation. "My wife and I want the boy. We've already got five of our own, but we still want Danny. He's our blood and he's got no one but us," he stated with undeniable sincerity.

"Does Danny know you want him?" Andrea demanded, unable to stay silent a second longer. "Children don't run away for no reason."

Burt gave her a straight look. "I ain't got a lot of schooling, lady, and not much money, either. But I love my family and Helen's a good wife and mother. We didn't mistreat Danny then and we won't. It's just he doesn't know us and losing his family like he did has got 'im scared." He glanced at Nick. "That's why he's not talking, or at least that's what his doc told us 'fore we left Williamsburg with him." He sighed, his lined face bearing mute testimony to his hard life. "Check with the police if you don't believe us. They asked us enough questions—"

"I'm not trying to imply that you would hurt Danny," Andrea interrupted hastily. She hesitated, then plunged ahead. "Your nephew has become very important to me in the short time I've had him." She glanced apologetically at Helen. "I'm worried about him."

Helen stared at her, tears filling her eyes. "I was so afraid when we realized he was missing. With all the kooks around today, anything could've happened to him," she confessed shakily. "Thank God you're the one who found him." Her voice broke on a sob as she covered her face with her hands.

Without thought Andrea went to her, gathering the weeping woman in her arms like a child. Her eyes caught Nick's over Helen's bowed head. The tender approval mixed with masculine sympathy in his gaze reached out to enfold her in an invisible embrace.

"Let's go get Danny," he suggested quietly to the man at his side. He sensed Burt's need to do something physical as an outlet for his own anxiety.

Burt seized gratefully on the diversion. "Helen will feel a lot better when she sees for herself the boy's okay," he agreed gruffly as he followed Nick out the door.

Andrea felt the loss of Nick's presence almost immediately, yet she had no time to dwell on her needs. She had to concentrate on helping Helen regain control before Danny saw his aunt.

"Ssh," she crooned, trying to absorb the shudders tearing at Helen. "He's all right."

"It's all my fault. I never thought to count heads when we stopped at the rest area," Helen gasped jerkily. "We were trying to get home...couldn't afford another night in a motel." She made a visible effort to bite back her sobs when she lifted her eyes to Andrea's. "We were all so tired." Andrea read the plea for understanding in the agonized depths. She squeezed her shoulders comfortingly. "It's over." The sound of her words echoed in her ears, sending a sharp pain through her. She had a sudden need to cry herself. But who would hold her? Who would reassure her everything was all right?

She eased away from Helen while thrusting her emotions aside for the moment. She didn't dare let go now. There would be time enough when Scrap— Danny was gone.

"Thank you for caring," Helen whispered, her expression conveying far more than simple words.

Andrea rose, aware of a fleeting wish Helen Dillion could have been the neglectful surrogate mother she had first envisioned. Then somehow she could have taken care of Danny herself. The instant the selfish thought was born, she suppressed it.

"Anyone would have," she denied quickly, taking a swift turn around the room. "He's a spirited boy, a real fighter. Any woman would be proud to name him hers." She glanced at the front door, wishing Nick would hurry. She needed to get out of the whole situation.

Nothing was as it should be. It wasn't supposed to hurt like this. After all, Danny was only a strange child that had entered her life for a few short days. He could never be hers, not by blood nor adoption.

The sounds of footsteps on her porch froze her in the restless pacing. She lifted her head to stare at the entrance. A second later Danny catapulted over the threshold to throw himself at her. She caught him in her arms as he wrapped around her to cling like a limpet. The tremors shaking his thin body told of his mute weeping.

"Damn," she swore softly, her gaze catching Burt's concerned expression and Helen's shocked hurt at her nephew's reaction. She barely noticed Burt going to comfort his wife as she focused on Nick. Help me, she begged silently. Now what should she do?

Nick saw her plea and the helpless look in her eyes. Unable to resist either, he moved toward her. "Give him to me," he commanded huskily. He felt her pain at the impending parting as his own. But there was nothing he could do. Danny had to be their first consideration.

Andrea released Danny into Nick's arms while retaining a hold on one small hand.

"Danny, look at me," she ordered, deliberately toughening her voice. Danny raised his head, his eyes shimmering with tears. "You're hurting your family and they love you. They've been very worried about you." She paused, letting her words sink in. "Now they've come to take you to your new home."

He shook his head vehemently. Clinging to her hand and Nick's neck, he stiffened in a physical refusal to accept her words. Andrea was conscious of everyone in the room and their total attention. She'd never felt more inadequate in her life, but she had to make Danny understand.

"You can't live with me, Danny. I have no home to offer you. I'm always on the road. You need schools, baseball games and friends. I can't give you that. Much as I like you and care about you, I can't take the place of your family." She stared at him, willing him to accept the truth. She desperately wanted to hold him in her arms, but she couldn't. He belonged to someone else.

Suddenly, without warning Danny snatched his hand from hers before wiggling to be free of Nick's arms. The moment his feet touched the floor, he ran for the open door and clamored down the steps to the Dillions' station wagon without a backward look. He got in and slumped dejectedly down in the rear seat.

Andrea gazed through the doorway, her eyes drinking in the last sight she would probably have of the child she had so quickly come to love. She barely heard Nick shepherd the Dillions outside nor did the sound of the old motor starting really impinge on her consciousness. All she could see or hear were Danny's footsteps as he left.

"Andrea?" Nick touched her arm lightly, curbing his uneasiness at her rigid attention on the departing car. There wasn't a sign of emotion on her face, but he had the feeling that she was shattering into a thousand pieces inside. "Come, let's sit down," he suggested, gently guiding her to one of the armchairs.

"Why does it hurt so much?" she breathed, scarcely aware she spoke her anguish aloud.

Nick settled down into the chair, pulling Andrea into his lap. He knew in this moment she was blind to him and his actions. She was locked away in her own private prison. He recognized and accepted her feelings, having experienced the same thing over one or two of the children he had brought to Seven Oaks. There was nothing he could do to help her. He could only hold her next to his heart and offer her the solace of his touch.

"For a moment, I wanted to hate them for taking him," she admitted, raising her eyes to his. The warm sympathy and understanding in his gaze triggered the tears that had been threatening for what seemed like forever. "Dammit. I don't know anything about children. Why do I want to keep him with me?" She choked back a sob, staring at his face through misty eyes.

"Because you love him," he answered simply before cradling her head against his shoulder. "He needed you and you were there for him. You protected him, clothed him and fed him. For a fleeting space of time he was yours."

The soothing cadence of Nick's voice poured over Andrea's ravaged senses to release the restraint she had placed on her emotions. One by one, tears welled, then overflowed in an ever increasing stream. Tiny gasps became sobs until suddenly she was crying out her pain in the haven of Nick's arms.

Nick held her, cuddling her slender body without making any attempt to stem the anguished outpouring. If he had ever doubted her femininity, he did no longer. His image of the tough lady truck driver was gone forever. Her capacity for gentleness and caring, for giving of herself to another person was revealed in the depth of her sorrow. She was all woman in his arms. Her strength he'd always known, yet even that had a new dimension. His hold tightened as he drew her closer, oddly glad she was allowing him to comfort her. The tempest was slowly burning itself out, he realized as her cries were gradually reduced to faint sniffles and a hiccup or two.

"Better?" he asked gently.

Andrea nodded, too empty, too drained to contemplate moving. In other circumstances she would have felt awkward at her position. Yet somehow being held in Nick's arms had not embarrassed her. It seemed so right to lean on him for a moment.

"You can visit him, you know. Both Helen and Burt invited us," he commented after a moment.

Andrea didn't hesitate. "No, it's better for Danny this way. If I keep our ties alive, it will only make it harder for him to settle down." She lifted her head to study him. "Don't you think so?"

"I agree." His lips curved into a faint smile, his eyes rich in emotion. "You're one special lady." He touched her cheek with his forefinger, lightly tracing one silvery tear trail. "Many would've taken the other choice, never counting the cost."

She, who never blushed, found heat stealing into her cheeks at his words. She couldn't think of a thing to say, even when his husky laughter filled her ears with surprising warmth.

Nick slipped his hand to her nape, unable to resist the appeal of her pink confusion and tear-damp eyes. "Honey, you're the most intriguing creature I've ever known," he whispered as his lips closed over hers. His hands, feeling strangely awkward, moved gently over her slim back.

Andrea parted her lips for his eager tongue to explore her inner sweetness. His palms kneaded her shoulders while he drank thirstily from the bounty that she offered. She heard him utter a groan deep in his throat as his muscles tautened against her. In spite of the thickness of the clothes between them, she was conscious of his arousal. A brief frisson of fear ran through her at the passion building between them. She had never known such desire nor been its object.

Then, incredibly, she felt him tremble and she knew it was his need of her that had shaken him. Her own fear vanished like smoke on the wind. A surge of joyous power flowed through her. She wanted him. The silent shout of exultation lit purple flames in her eyes as she cradled him to her.

He buried his lips against her throat, his breathing hard and shallow. "I want you," he rasped hoarsely. He lifted his head to stare at her with an unaccustomed vulnerability in his expression. "Let me love you. Let me take away the emptiness if only for a little while.''

Enchanted by the poignancy of his plea, Andrea nodded. ''Yes, please,'' she whispered, reinforcing her gesture. She met his eyes, knowing her inexperience showed. ''Tell me what to do.''

He shook his head, his expression going from passionate urgency to incredible tenderness. ''The next time, love. Let me pleasure you now.'' He rose, somehow continuing to hold her in his arms. He cradled her against his chest as he strode to her bedroom.

Sunlight cast lacy tracings over the room as he set her on her feet beside the bed. ''Stay here,'' he commanded softly. ''And close your eyes.''

Andrea did as he asked, too surprised to question his curious request. The sounds of him moving about mingled with the rustle of fabric and a muting of the glare penetrating her eyelids.

''Now,'' he breathed, tilting her chin with one finger.

Andrea opened her eyes to survey her transformed bedroom. Drawn drapes shut out the day to create a cool haven of silence. The covers on her bed were turned back invitingly to reveal smooth sheets and fluffy pillows.

''You're beautiful.'' Nick placed a kiss on her slightly parted lips. He smiled into her bemused eyes as his hands drifted to her shoulders. For a moment they lingered, offering her an escape if she chose to take it.

Andrea stared at him, losing sight of everything but his expression. Desire, tenderness, passion all lay revealed for her to see. "Nick," she murmured, unknowingly voicing the plea of her body and her mind.

As if her words were the signal he waited for, he slipped his hands down to deftly undo the buttons of her shirt. A second later, he dropped the blouse on the floor before beginning to unfasten her jeans. Soon, they, too, joined her garment on the carpet.

Mesmerized by his tender concentration, Andrea stood unmoving as her bra and panties followed the pattern. When she stood naked before him, he stepped back to remove his clothes down to his briefs.

Her eyes widened with each golden inch of flesh he exposed. His sleek contours held a grace refined to the point of beauty. When he lifted her in his arms and lay her on her bed, she felt the warmth of him surround her.

He came down beside her, brushing back the midnight curls from her forehead. "Comfortable?" he murmured softly.

"Yes," she answered back, amazed at the deep cadence of her voice.

"I'm not going to do anything you don't like. I want to make this very special for you." His hands caressed her shoulders soothingly, yet in ever increasing circles. "Your skin is like golden satin." His fingertips swept over the aching fullness of her breasts in a slow arc.

Andrea inhaled deeply as the languid stroking continued with almost lazy patterns. Heat filled her, demanding she move. She arched up as he drew his thumbs carefully across her pouting nipples.

"Nick." The plea of earlier was no longer. Instead she demanded more. She needed him.

His lips curved in pleasure at her calling of his name. He cupped her breasts, tactilely adoring their lush curves. "Delicious," he said hoarsely, his lips pressing tiny kisses on her throat.

His mouth covered hers in a hot, liquid kiss. All the while his hands traced magic circles of sensations over her body, drifting downward with every touch.

His head slowly lowered to one taut nipple in a delicate caress that caused a shudder of sheer desire to run through her. His tongue saluted each breast before he glanced up, his aquamarine eyes drawing her into a sensuous sea of pleasure. As if reassured by the drugged languor of her expression, he bent his head once again to suckle at the tender twins of femininity awaiting him.

Andrea made a sound that was half moan, half gasp. She slid her arms around his neck and pulled him to her in a fierce possessiveness she was barely aware of in the swirling passion of the moment. Nick's lips glided over her breasts to her stomach at the second his hand slipped into the ebony thicket hiding the essence of her femininity.

Andrea writhed beneath the dual claiming, vibrantly alive to every breath he took, every move he made. Tension filled her, demanding release. "Love me, Nick," she pleaded, knowing with an instinct old as time itself that he could free her from the web he had spun.

"Gladly, love," he breathed huskily. He moved away for an instant to remove his last covering. Then he spread her legs gently and eased his weight onto her body.

Andrea accepted him eagerly, pushing against his hard flesh in an effort to hurry their union. He gentled her with words and his touch before delicately, inch by inch, fusing their bodies as one.

Feeling unbelievably treasured by the careful invasion, Andrea was in awe of his control and his concern for her untouched state. Every muscle and nerve in her seemed to be pulsating with a need only the man above her could satisfy. Yet in that moment, she knew she would never forget his tenderness.

Then he moved, slowly at first to give her a chance to catch the rhythm of their mating dance. All thought ceased as the ancient ritual unfolded in all its glory.

Andrea lost track of how long the spiral of desire and fulfillment continued. She arched at Nick's whispered urgings. Her hands and lips caressed him in a need to give him a measure of the delight he offered her. Higher she pushed, deeper she drew him to her until suddenly the dam burst within her. She cried out his name as the liquid rush left her trembling in his arms as he surged to replace what she had given him.

Nick's breath was coming in little jerks, his heart beating a wild melody of his satisfaction. "Andrea," he rasped, his words stirring the soft tendrils of hair at her temple. "Beautiful."

Andrea drank in his voice silently echoing his description in her mind. She wanted to tell him how wonderful he had made her first time, but she couldn't get even that much out. She felt too weak, too fluid to lift her hand. She was quivering in his arms and unable to still the small tremors.

Without releasing her, Nick rolled over so they were facing each other, before drawing the coverlet up to enclose them in a snug cocoon. He slid his arms around her to press their still-bound bodies into deeper intimacy.

"Don't regret this," he pleaded, his eyes searching hers. "I've never known a woman who could give so much. Be proud of your passion."

Startled at his strange gravity, Andrea stared down at him. "I don't understand," she murmured, feeling a faint flicker of unease.

"You were vulnerable, we both know it," he clarified, the words seeming to be drawn out of him against his will. "I'd rather you'd hate me for making love to you than feel guilty for sharing yourself with me."

"I couldn't hate you," she denied instantly. "Never that." She paused briefly, unsure if she should continue. "I wanted you and I needed you to make me forget," she admitted with painful honesty. "I'm glad it was you. You made me feel wonderful."

Nick inhaled deeply, knowing a lightening of the intolerable burden of his own conscience. He had been so afraid he'd see regret in her eyes when she realized what they had done. But the amethyst depths held no shadows now, only a vivid sparkle of life and the special awareness of a woman's power. The knowledge he had been with her on her voyage of discovery filled him with pride and a deep need to be the only one she gave herself to. His arms tightened at the thought. Too soon, his mind warned before his mouth could form the words.

She was a spirit at home traveling the land. He wanted to hold her close, but could she survive the clipping of her wings? Did he have the right to even ask it of her?

Andrea sensed the tension invading their embrace. Something was wrong. "Nick?" she questioned, watching him closely for a clue.

Mentally forcing his doubts aside, Nick sought the refuge of her touch. For now he would be content with whatever she would grant him. "It's nothing, honey," he whispered deeply, drawing her lips to his.

Reassured by the look in his eyes and the desire they shared, she gave herself up to the magic enchantment he created. She knew there could come a time when she would examine her actions, but today she would revel in this new world he had shown her.

Seven

Andrea slipped between her sheets after darting a quick look at her bedside clock. It was late. Every muscle in her body ached with the tension and emotions of the day, yet she never felt less like sleeping. Nick was gone. Danny was gone. And she was left behind with a mind full of questions, half-formed feelings and few answers.

The only relief on the horizon was Nick's plans to return the next weekend. She had hated saying goodbye to him, she admitted, as she stared at her darkened ceiling. Now in the privacy of her room, she could freely acknowledge her need of him. He had awakened the passionate side of her nature with gentleness and consideration. But more importantly, he had understood her attachment to Danny far better than her own family had done.

Though Big Jack and her brothers had been sympathetic, it had been Nick who had postponed his trip home so he could take her out to lunch. He had filled her afternoon with pleasure, holding at bay the sadness and pain Danny's repudiation had created. They had shared a meal while exchanging conversation about their backgrounds. Afterward they had driven out to Quabbin Reservoir and walked through the woods, just talking. He had made her laugh with his dry wit, he had moved her with tales of his children at Seven Oaks, but most of all he had given her a glimpse of himself.

She smiled gently in the darkness, remembering the silences that had been almost as eloquent as their words. Did all lovers share an unspoken rapport, she wondered, or was it something special just reserved for them?

She rolled on her side, her eyes peering through the shadow at the unfamiliar shape leaning against her far wall. A baseball bat! Danny! She gasped at the emptiness that the sight reminded her existed now that he was gone. She had bought him that. Her gaze traced the clearly defined silhouette. Nick had bought him the glove and ball that lay on the floor nearby. Tears welled in her eyes as she remembered his happiness at their joint gift, a gift he had forgotten to take with him and one that she would never enjoy with him.

Restless, Andrea tossed back the covers. She wiped her fingers across her damp cheeks as she padded over to the forlorn and forsaken present, silently awaiting a child's hands to use it.

She bent to pick up the baseball mitt just as the phone shrilled in the silence. She jerked upright, startled at the intrusion. She moved to her bedside table, a frown pleating her forehead. She lifted the receiver while switching on the lamp beside the phone. Soft golden light filled the bedroom as Nick's voice caressed her ear. Her expression cleared instantly, a smile bringing pleasure instead of pain to her features.

"Hi," she murmured softly, sinking onto the edge of the bed. Her unhappiness over Danny was forgotten for the moment in the delight of his unexpected contact.

"Honey, I'm sorry to be ringing so late," he began.

Andrea interrupted, fiercely glad he had cared enough to call her. The emptiness of the night was gone, so too was her restlessness. "I wasn't asleep," she replied, her voice husky from her earlier tears.

Nick inhaled sharply at her admission. "I wish I were there with you," he muttered.

Hearing the rough concern in his tone, Andrea felt a sudden flicker of fear. "What is it?" she demanded.

"It's Danny. He's run away again," he replied tersely. "Sometime between nine and ten this evening."

Andrea swore, something she rarely did. "Have they notified the police?" She shook her head impatiently at her own inane question. "Scratch that?" she mumbled. "Where would he go?" Her mind instantly filled with images of the child lost and alone, unable to speak. It was a horrifying vision.

"Helen and Burt think he's heading your way. The police found a woman who gave him a ride to the interstate."

"My way?" Andrea echoed with a short crack of unamused laughter. "After the way he left, I think I'm the last one he wants to see." She gripped the receiver tightly, trying without success to suppress the memories of the small hand snatched from hers, the angry look of dislike and disappointment on the too thin boyish face. "Hitchhiking," she groaned as the last part of Nick's words penetrated. "Oh God, he isn't."

"He is," Nick confirmed grimly. "You aren't out there this time to help him."

Andrea stared into space, seeing nothing. Her first instinct was to get in her Mustang and head for Boston. But she knew she had little chance of finding one seven-year-old child in all the miles stretching between the two cities.

"I'm going to get on the CB base. We'll find him," she decided abruptly. "I'll call you back as soon as I finish sending out the alert."

Nick didn't waste time demanding explanations or on useless words of reassurance. With a quick promise to stay by the phone, he hung up. Andrea was slipping out of her lavender nightgown before she had replaced the receiver. She threw on her clothes in seconds, then raced up the path to the main house. The base CB was set up in the back room off the kitchen.

Andrea entered the functionally furnished area, barely pausing in her stride to switch on the lights and the citizen's band. Dialing the channel most of her trucker buddies used, she keyed the mike.

"Breaker, breaker, you got the Purple Flash hunting up any eighteen-wheeler jockey on the interstate heading Boston way."

"You got the Delaware Dragster, come on back."

Andrea breathed a sigh of relief at the familiar handle. She and Dell had run together more than once.

"Delaware, I need a favor. There's a boy hiking from Boston. He's seven years old and his name is Danny. He's mute, with brown hair, green eyes, a smallish build. I want him picked up by one of us. Can you pass the word?" Static greeted her ears as she waited for her friend's reply.

"Gotcha, Flash." He quickly repeated her description. "I'll let the east- and west-bounders know right away. We'll give you a shout as soon as we have anything."

Andrea thanked him, then signed off. She sprawled limply in her chair, knowing she had done all she could. In a matter of minutes the airwaves would be sizzling with her message as each trucker received and passed along her plea. From their elevated vantage point, countless eyes would be scanning the roadway many knew as well as their own backyards. If Danny was out there, one of the "Knights of the Road" would find him.

"Andy?"

At the sound of her name, Andrea jerked around to find her father standing in the doorway. His mussed gray hair and haphazardly tied bathrobe attested to his disturbed sleep.

"Sorry I woke you," she apologized automatically.

He dismissed her words with a wave of his hand. "I heard the call you sent out." He ambled toward her, his strong, stocky build bearing the experience of his years and a calm certainty that Andrea found infinitely comforting. "That was a smart move."

She inclined her head, accepting his compliment without really hearing it. "I've got to call Nick and let him know."

"Nick?" Big Jack glanced at her sharply. "What's he got to do with this?"

Andrea paused briefly to meet her father's shrewd eyes. "He's the one who called me about Danny," she explained while she finished dialing. Nick answered on the first ring, his voice harsh with worry.

"The alert's going out now. I'll let you know the second I hear anything."

"I wish I were with you, honey," he rasped heavily. "Waiting alone is damnably hard."

Warmed by his concern, Andrea lost some of the loneliness of her self-appointed vigil. Just knowing he wanted to share her anxiety made the hours ahead a little less painful. Nothing could lessen her fears for Danny, but Nick's support went a long way toward making them more bearable.

Forgetting her father's presence, Andrea gave in to the need to tell him what she was feeling. "I'm glad you're with me in this." A faint oath, barely stifled sounded in her ear.

Nick cleared his throat. "I'm going over to the Dillions. Call me there when you hear something or if you need me."

Once again their goodbyes were minimal. Andrea stared at the phone sitting so innocently beside the CB. Both were lifelines of a sort, one to a network of friends looking for a child and the other to a man who had given her so much in such a short time.

"I'll fix us some coffee," Big Jack offered quietly.

Andrea lifted her head to find her father watching her closely. "You don't have to stay up with me," she murmured.

He shrugged his massive shoulders. "Something tells me I'd better make use of your unexpected presence around here," he returned in an odd tone.

Andrea tipped her chin, wondering at the hidden messages she detected in his comment. But before she could question him, a breaker for the Flash came over the CB. Grabbing the mike, she answered swiftly only to receive a report that everyone had been alerted but so far no one had seen Danny.

Minutes ticked by as she and Big Jack kept their silent vigil. Periodically calls came in but always with the same result. No one had seen Danny.

"More coffee?" Big Jack asked, collecting their empty mugs.

Andrea shook her head. "Not for me. I'm floating now." She glared at the electronic marvel that had produced so many words and no answers. "Why hasn't someone spotted him yet?'' she muttered in frustration. She raked a hand through her tousled black curls, wishing she could do something. Anything was better than sitting idly by, sipping coffee.

"Relax, Andy," Big Jack commanded, his expression sympathetic. He laid a blunt-fingered hand on her shoulder. "They'll find him for you."

Andrea raised agonized eyes to his. "But when? It had been more than three hours since Nick notified us. Boston is barely that far away."

"I know." He sighed, suddenly losing a bit of his rugged vitality. "Hang in there." He patted her shoulder before giving her an encouraging smile. "How about a brandy to help you to relax?"

Andrea grimaced. Not even in a situation like this would she drink that vile tasting cognac. It might be her father's favorite late night tipple, but it definitely wasn't hers and he knew it. "No thanks," she drawled, seeing through his ploy to divert her mind. She wrinkled her nose expressively, unable to ignore his effort to lighten her mood. She knew he was trying to help in the only way he could.

He grinned, looking absurdly pleased at her reaction. "Don't insult good liquor," he shot back on his way to the door.

Andrea kept an answering smile on her face until he was out of sight. Then she slumped dejectedly back in her chair. How much longer, she railed silently. A second later the CB shrilled to life, jerking her upright.

"Breaker, breaker, come on Purple Flash. Come back to Ratchet Randy."

"You got the Purple Flash," she replied with forced evenness. She was afraid to let herself believe the excitement she heard in the unknown voice.

"I got your boy, Flash."

Andrea's eyes widened as Randy rattled off his location and asked her to meet him at the Springfield exit off the interstate nearest her home.

"Hurray!" she shouted exuberantly the moment she signed off. She twirled around the room, too relieved to sit still.

Big Jack came hurrying in, his face going from worried to delighted on observing her antics. "I take it Danny's okay," he commented, making no secret of his own relief.

She nodded as she grabbed the phone to let Nick and the Dillions know. "I'll bring him to you," Andrea offered moments later after Helen awkwardly thanked her.

"I couldn't let you do that," the older woman protested uncomfortably.

Andrea frowned, easily guessing the strain another trip would place on the family, both financially and emotionally. "I was coming over tomorrow to visit Nick anyway," Andrea explained hurriedly, mentally crossing her fingers that Nick wouldn't give her lie away.

"You were?" Helen questioned doubtfully but with barely masked hope.

"I was," she affirmed before adding, "Let me speak to Nick. With Danny with me, I'll be starting out a little later than I'd planned." She waited, hoping her assurance would calm Helen. The snatches of conversation on the other end of the line indicated that at least part of her ploy had worked.

"Andrea?"

Nick's voice flowed over her, his tone subtly conveying his curiosity about what was going on. "Don't talk. Just listen," Andrea commanded, wasting no time with the niceties. "Helen and Burt are upset enough without having to worry about coming after Danny. I offered to bring him to Boston and you heard her answer. So I lied. I told her I was coming to town anyway to see you. I told her I'd be getting a late start because of Danny. Will you back me up?" Suddenly realizing how presumptuous her demand sounded, Andrea bit her lip to stifle a groan of self-disgust.

"Honey, of course, in this case I don't mind if you're delayed. My housekeeper will let you into the apartment whenever you arrive if I'm still at the office." He paused before chuckling with seeming indulgence.

Andrea's eyes widened at the definitely masculine sensuality of the gesture. What was he up to? she wondered distractedly. He was making it sound as though the two of them would be sharing his place during her visit.

"I'm not going to stay with you," Andrea managed finally. "It was only a cover story."

"I know, sweetheart, but it can't be helped," he agreed with silky softness.

Andrea rolled her eyes heavenward in exasperation at his ability to answer her and continue to foster the illusion he was creating for the Dillions.

"Nick Griffin, I am *not* staying with you," she muttered irritably.

"I'll expect you by noon," Nick warned in a lover's tone. "Drive carefully."

Before Andrea could draw another breath the dial tone sounded in her ear. "That man," she swore, flinging the receiver she held down. There had been an unmistakable note of amusement in Nick's voice. But had there been something else hidden in the fluid cadence? He had sounded so sincere, so believable.

"What's wrong, Andy?"

Andrea swung around, suddenly remembering her father's presence. "I'll be taking Danny back to Boston tomorrow—" she paused, correcting herself "—no, I mean today."

One iron-gray brow rose at her neutral inflection. "And?" he prompted.

"And," she repeated, knowing Big Jack had caught the controlled note and wondered at it. She was never restrained about anything and he knew it. "You heard."

He inclined his head, a teasing glint in his deep blue eyes. "I take it Nick's holding you to your small truth-stretching."

Andrea dropped into her chair, glaring at her parent. "Don't look so pleased. I did it to help the Dillions."

Big Jack strolled over to the desk to perch on one corner. He stared down at his offspring. "I'd say you and Nick settled your differences over the weekend."

Andrea started at the accuracy of his assessment. "So?" she asked, wondering what more, if anything, her father had noticed.

"So the man obviously wants to see more of you. And you, my gypsy, have just handed him a ready-made way to do it." He grinned openly at her annoyed expression.

"I thought fathers were supposed to protect their daughters from the big bad male wolf," she shot back, feeling goaded by his attitude. The fact that it was just possible that he was right was an added spur to her temper.

Big Jack tipped his head in a gesture Andrea recognized as one of consideration. Seconds ticked by before he met her eyes, his own clear with his belief.

"You're an unusual woman, daughter of mine. Part of what you are is a result of your upbringing, but most of it is just you. I've always tried to be there when and if you needed me or my support, but I've never tried to run your life. I'm not starting now. You're strong enough to handle anything or anyone you choose. You've got an integrity most people would find difficult to live up to. But you're also sensitive. In short, Andrea, I trust you to know what you want and if you make a mistake, I know you'll deal with that, too. I make no judgments other than to tell you I like Nick as a man.''

Stunned at her father's comprehensive accolade, Andrea gazed at him in silence. They had always shared a very special rapport. He had understood her need to wander, even when her brothers had condemned her choice as idiotic and downright impulsive. He had helped her finance the purchase of her own rig and later even understood her need to buy the back cottage from him. And now, once again, he was showing his ability to read her needs. He neither condemned nor condoned; instead he left her to find her own way.

"I love you, Pop," she murmured, her eyes bright with the force of her emotions.

"I love you, Flash," he rumbled, leaning forward to drop a kiss on her forehead. He rose, casting a look at the silent CB. "Why don't you go pack while I wait for our friend Randy to call us?"

Realizing that he was vaguely embarrassed at his eloquence, Andrea got obediently to her feet. "Good idea," she agreed, heading for the door. "You'll phone me when you hear?"

He nodded before seating himself in the chair she just vacated. He picked up one of Ned's hunting magazines and started to read. Andrea studied his broad back for a moment, trying to come to terms with what he had said.

It was almost as if he realized she and Nick were lovers. But how could he? She could barely take in the extreme shift in their relationship herself. Shaking her head over the unanswerable thoughts whirling in her mind, she left the main house. She entered her cottage uncertain how her life had suddenly become so mixed up.

Nick, Danny, her new feelings about her job—each one had complicated her simple existence beyond recognition. Each had brought fulfillment in its own way, but still something was missing. Some vital ingredient to bring the whole picture into focus.

She efficiently packed her case with clothes enough for a few days. With her three weeks off, she could have stayed longer but she still doubted her presence would help Danny settle.

Danny! In her bewilderment over Nick, she had almost forgotten her small waif. Why had he been coming to her? After the way he had left earlier, it just didn't seem logical that he would seek her out. Yet that's what he had done. Randy had stated plainly that Danny had carried a hand-printed card with her address on it.

Thinking about the nameless demons that had to be haunting him, Andrea stared off into space. Why didn't he speak? Had he seen something or felt something that was so traumatic that his subconscious had robbed him of his voice?

The phone rang, intruding into her thoughts. Andrea snapped the locks on the case with one hand while lifting the receiver with the other.

"He's about fifteen minutes away from the exit," Big Jack announced without wasting a second on extra words.

Andrea was equally brief. "Okay, I'm on my way."

A few moments later she eased her restored '66 Mustang down the drive and onto the virtually deserted street. She flipped her CB on, easily selecting Randy's channel as she drove. Taking full advantage of the lightly trafficked streets, Andrea edged right up to the speed limit. She wanted to delay her helpful truckin' buddy as little as possible with his errand of mercy. She arrived at the appointed pickup point with three minutes to spare.

She scanned the exit ramp for a sign of Randy's rig before keying her mike to hail her friend. His answer preceded the appearance of his eighteen-wheeler by seconds.

Andrea got out as he pulled to a stop behind her car in the parking area of the service plaza. She hardly had time to reach the cab of the dark brown truck before a small figure climbed down and hurled himself at her.

Her arms closed automatically around Danny's thin frame as she raised her eyes to the lanky man in western garb walking toward her.

"He's the one you want?" the newcomer queried.

"Yes, and thanks," Andrea replied gratefully.

He touched his cowboy hat with a forefinger. "Anytime, Flash. I was kinda glad I could help just so's I could meet'cha," he drawled. "Big Jack's daughter's got quite a rep." He extended his hand.

Andrea took it, unsurprised at the man's words. Her father was well known on the east coast and, after a decade of driving, so was she.

"Keep the rubber side down, friend," she offered in goodbye as he released her.

"You too, Flash."

Andrea glanced down at Danny as Randy left. She brushed back the tousled hair from his forehead before unwrapping his arms from her waist. She lifted him away slightly so she could see his face. The defiant expression on his weary features couldn't hide his need for her. She knew she should scold him but she just couldn't bring herself to do it tonight. He had had enough for one day.

She smiled gently as she took his hand. "Come on, Scrapper, let's go home and get us some shut-eye," she drawled.

Eight

Andrea switched her attention from the crowded highway before her to the silent child at her side. With every mile closer to Boston, Danny had become more apprehensive. At the start of the journey, he had been interested in the constant CB chatter and the scenery along the interstate. Yet now nothing seemed to deflect his rigidly focused gaze on the city skyline. She wanted to reassure him about his future, but she had no idea how. The only thing she could do was divert him.

"You know, Danny, Boston is one of my favorite towns. I've seen a lot of them, too," she added conversationally. She glanced back to the road while still monitoring his reaction closely. "There's so much to see here. There's a model of the *Constitution* docked at the Charleston Navy Yard. You'll probably hear about that ship in one of your school classes.'' The faint brightening in Danny's expression as he peered ahead prompted her to continue. ''The *Constitution* is the oldest commissioned ship in the Navy and it's got forty-four guns. It's really something to tour.'' She hesitated, searching her memory for more bits of information that might appeal to him. ''Did you know the Boston Tea Party took place here? You remember that's when a bunch of colonists dressed up like Indians and boarded the English ships. They dumped a whole cargo of tea overboard to protest the tax the king was demanding.''

Danny patted her arm to get her attention. Andrea glanced at him as he held two fingers behind his head, like feathers. She smiled, relieved at the curiosity in his eyes. The idea of grown-ups dressing in Indian garb obviously appealed to him.

''If you like the Indians, I bet you'd love Paul Revere. He started his ride to Lexington from here. He's the one who warned the colonists that the Redcoats were coming.'' She chuckled at his quick mime of a man bouncing up and down on a horse. Seeing his interest was truly caught, Andrea kept up a stream of information on his new home. She described Quincy Market, Boston Common and street festivals in the summer in Boston's North End.

By the time she eased to a stop in front of a modest apartment house in the South End section of the city,

Danny was far more at ease. She took his hand as they started up the walk, giving him an encouraging smile.

"Now, remember, I gave you my address and Nick's. You don't need to hitchhike anymore. It's dangerous. We're both going to be around, so there's no need to worry." She studied him unobtrusively as they climbed the uncarpeted stairs. "Remember your promise. No more running away," she repeated sternly. "Okay?"

Danny squeezed her hand, his expression earnest as he nodded his agreement. He pointed to the door ahead marked 402.

"That's it," she agreed, answering his silent question. On impulse, she bent down to gather his small body in her arms. "They want to love you, Scrapper, if you'll just let them," she whispered softly. She released him slowly, watching his green eyes for a sign of understanding. "All of us want you to be happy, but you have to want it, too."

He stared at her, neither rejecting nor accepting her claim. For a long moment, Andrea searched his face, hoping for a clue to what was going on in his mind. There was none. Sighing softly at her inability to interpret his feelings, Andrea rose. She would have to be content with his promise not to run away, it appeared.

She took his hand again before walking the last few paces to the Dillions' door. She only had time to knock once before the panel opened to reveal Helen, her brown eyes reflecting her anxiety and relief. For seconds neither spoke as the older woman stared at her nephew. Then she lifted her head, her hand going nervously to her short cap of chocolate waves.

"Please come in," she murmured awkwardly with a swift look at Danny.

Correctly interpreting Helen's discomfort, Andrea smiled in an effort to relieve the tension of the meeting. She followed Helen to the living room and took a seat on the gold tweed sofa. She glanced around appreciatively at the inexpensive, yet attractively furnished area. All of the furniture showed definite signs of use, yet there was an air of love and pride in the crisp white curtains and carefully placed knick-knacks.

"You have a beautiful home," she commented sincerely. She gestured toward the house plants lining two tiers of unfinished boards under the window. "And a green thumb, too." She grinned companionably. "Mine's black. I couldn't grow anything even if it came equipped with complete directions."

Helen's lips curved upward in a tentative response to her words. "My two oldest children are always bringing me cuttings. I never have quite figured out where they get them all." She gestured to the primitive shelf supported by brown painted building blocks. "They even got the wood and those bricks for me from a house that was being torn down in the neighborhood." She gazed at the primitive creation as though it were a valued antique.

Andrea was touched deeply by the love glowing in Helen's eyes. Once again she damned herself for the hasty conclusions about the Dillions. If it weren't for the obvious scarcity of funds and the drain Danny would place on the already burdened family, she would be totally sure about leaving him here. As it was she had to accept the situation, but she couldn't help wondering how the Dillions could afford the care Danny's speech problem and its emotional cause would require. She couldn't shake the feeling that he needed more than they would be able to give him. She hoped Nick would think of something as he promised. Forcing her personal beliefs aside for the moment, Andrea tried to draw Danny and Helen closer together. By the time she took her leave an hour later, Danny and his aunt were more at ease, although neither could have been described as relaxed.

Andrea guided her car through Boston's busy streets, turning the problem of Danny over in her mind. There had to be a better solution than the present one. Danny had too many problems for a family like the Dillions. Even she could see he needed specialized help. For one thing, there had to be more of a reason for his continued silence than just the upheaval of his life.

Once again she remembered Nick's offer to help the Dillions somehow as she turned her attention to the beautiful, gas-lit streets of Beacon Hill. Tree-lined sidewalks flowed by shuttered brick town houses. Here many of Boston's wealthy, socially prominent families had lived throughout the nineteenth century. Nick's town house was on Beacon Street overlooking the Commons. She whipped into a parking place just as another car eased out, blessing her luck at finding one of the rare slots unoccupied.

For a moment, she sat debating whether staying with Nick was such a good idea. Here amidst the stately homes she felt as out of place as a thistle in a rose garden. What did she know of the kind of life these old brick buildings had seen and probably still knew?

She sighed in resignation, aware that she had no choice but to enter the gleaming ebony door of Nick's house. She couldn't leave without knowing whether he had been able to secure the financial assistance the Dillions so desperately needed to help Danny. She deliberately ignored her own desire to see Nick again. She was determined to halt the strange growing need to have him near. She had tried telling herself it was only natural that her body remember its first lover. But what of her mind, that recklessly tenacious part so bent on recalling every moment of their time together?

She shivered as she walked the last few feet of red bricked sidewalk and mounted the two steps leading to the arched entranceway of the town house. She cleared her expression as she raised the shiny brass knocker and let it fall. The door swung open almost at the instant her arm returned to her side.

"Andrea," Nick greeted her, his eyes sweeping over her denim-clad form. His gaze lingered for a split second on the golden V framed at her throat by a blue-and-dusty rose plaid shirt.

Andrea felt the warm touch of his glance flow over her, bringing her senses to life at the sight and sound of him. She stared into his eyes, unable and unwilling to look away. When he took her hand to urge her inside, she obeyed blindly.

"I've argued my way around this attraction since you left," she confessed, when he turned to face her.

"Have you?" he asked, one golden brow quirking in mingled amusement and acceptance.

She nodded once. "It didn't work."

He caught her shoulders, drawing her against him with a gentle pressure that offered her an escape if she chose to take it. For a moment Andrea resisted, more because she was surprised by the hunger she saw in his expression than her own emotional confusion.

"Nick?" she questioned, curious, intrigued and oddly pleased by his desire.

"I've had a picture of you in my mind all morning." He stared at her intently, visually drinking in every curve and hollow of her face. "I should have been concentrating only on my work but I couldn't. Your scent, the feel of you and the taste of you haunted me." He framed her face with his hands. "Why?" He paused, his searching probe seeming to plunge past her outer appeal to the essence of her being. "Why now after all these years?"

Andrea traced her lips with her tongue, unsurprised at how easily he had voiced her own doubts. "I don't know," she whispered, wishing he had answers for both of them. Maybe then the should-I?-or-shouldn't-I? fog surrounding her would lift.

"I wasn't sure you'd stay with me," he admitted huskily. "I'm not even certain what made me urge you to accept my invitation."

Remembering the logical arguments he had used to counter her every objection when she had called him this morning to discuss his plan, Andrea's lips curved slightly. "Urged?" she echoed. "It felt more like coercion to me."

He bent his head until his mouth hovered a fingertip away. "I wanted you here," he rasped huskily. "Now I find I also want you to want to be here."

Andrea heard the plea in his voice. For a moment the emotional fog parted, and something in her demanded she reassure him. She neither understood nor could she name the urgency she felt, yet she couldn't deny its potency.

"I do want to be with you," she breathed in a throaty whisper. "You've haunted my hours, too. Even when Danny filled my thoughts, I could feel you in the secret corners of my mind, waiting for me."

Nick wrapped his arms around her, cradling her in a close embrace. Andrea slipped her hands under his suit coat and to his waist. Entwined as they were, she could feel the hard column of his thighs and knew a sudden, once familiar weakness in her own limbs. How strange that the touch of the heated muscles should make her feel so soft and melting in contrast.

"Andrea." Nick's voice was a velvet whisper against her lips as he covered her mouth with his. The first brush of his lips was light, almost tentative. He teased her with tiny kisses, wooing her, then persuading her into parting her lips for him. Quick to accept the silent invitation, his tongue plunged greedily into the inner sweetness with astonishing speed.

With a moan of pleasure and swiftly spiraling need, Andrea arched against him in an effort to lessen the nonexistent distance between them. Even as she responded so ardently to his touch, one part of her wondered at her uninhibited sensuality.

"I needed that," Nick groaned, breathing hard as he released her. "It was even better than I remembered." Then he was kissing her again.

"I know," she agreed dazedly while he caressed the sensitive hollow of her throat.

Somehow his hand was between them, cupping the aching fullness of one breast. "So soft and sweet."

"Nick," Andrea gasped, half in excitement and half in protest. "Your housekeeper," she whispered as his thumb lightly rasped across her tender nipple.

"Gone," he murmured. He lowered his head against the cushiony curve of her, rubbing his cheek back and forth over the twin ripe swells with a sensual, almost catlike contentment. "I never knew how good a woman could feel until you, honey."

No more than she had ever known how a man could feel, Andrea thought feverishly. The muscles of her throat and chest were so taut that every breath hurt. Every touch of Nick's body against hers left a trail of molten fire in its wake. But his passionate words—those were evocatively stimulating in a way she had never known.

When he lifted her in his arms, she was past thinking about anything or anyone but him. The stairs, another hall and a room in shades of blue passed in a haze of shape and color. The soft feel of velvet against her cheek when he lowered her onto his bed was only one more sensation to her heightened awareness.

His clothes seemed to melt away beneath her eager fingers even as he brushed her own aside. Then, bare as nature intended, they flowed together in a beautiful silence that spoke more eloquently than words. Breath mated with breath, softness to strength, man to woman, two became one. For a magical moment the world was brand new and colored with the deep rich fulfillment of passion satiated.

Andrea drifted in a languid sea of contentment in the aftermath of their loving. Her head on Nick's shoulder, her hand pressed against his heart, she inhaled the musky scent that was pure Nick.

"You go to my head, sweet witch," Nick murmured lazily, his fingers lightly stroking Andrea's slender back. "I've never ravished a woman on my doorstep before."

Andrea heard the puzzled wonder in his voice and smiled. Nick, the proper Bostonian, the disapproving friend of her brother, was definitely having a problem coming to grips with their changing relationship. It was reassuring to know she wasn't the only one going through the adjustment from what had been to what was now.

"I can't say I've ever been ravished before, either,"
she teased. She lightly traced the male nipple so close
to her lips. At his gasp, she raised her head.

Nick stared into her mischievous violet eyes. "She-
devil," he swore tenderly. "For an innocent, you learn
fast." He frowned, suddenly struck by his comment.
"I still can't believe you've never been seriously involved with anyone."

Amused by his elaborately offhand way of referring to her virginal state, she laughed softly. "I don't
see why," she parried, propping her chin on her hands.
She pressed her breasts against his naked chest to stare
at him interestedly.

Color ran up under his skin at her direct look as she
circled her lips with the tip of her tongue. The poetic
justice of watching him squirm, even a little bit after
all those years of disapproval, was intoxicating.

"Vagabonds usually don't light long enough to
form liaisons," she drawled, one ebony brow winging
up at an intriguing angle.

Nick's eyes flickered at the provocative expression.
Before she knew what was happening, Andrea found
herself flat on her back with Nick looming over her.

"That independent, devil-may-care streak of yours
is going to get you in trouble one day," he promised
with deep feeling.

Stunned by his quick return, Andrea froze beneath
him. She had only thought to pick at his Boston pro-
priety. She had never meant to irritate him. Yet why
should he be annoyed? she wondered, perplexed.

"Why does it matter?" she asked quickly. The sudden realization of her limited role in his life drove the words from her mouth. A shaft of pain pierced the cloud of fulfillment surrounding her.

"Don't look like that," Nick commanded, seeing the hurt in her eyes. "It matters because you're important to me. I've never cared before whether the woman I was with had had other lovers." He touched her lips with a gentle forefinger, tracing the ripe fullness with intense concentration. "I feel so possessive of you, it scares me. I want to hold you against my heart and never let you go." He lifted his eyes to hers, the blue-green depths alive with a rainbow of emotions. "But I can't hold you, can I? You've always run free. If I snatch what I want, I'll damage us both."

Andrea caught her breath at the hurt underlying his words and marring his expression. The depth of feeling he had revealed shocked her even as it filled her with warmth. "What are you saying, Nick?" she asked, afraid to interpret his statement. It would be so easy to let her own chaotic emotions color what he offered.

"I'm saying I want more than this. I want you in my life," he paused, clearly searching for a way to explain. "Everything's happened so fast, yet I feel like this moment's been coming since I first saw you with skinned knees."

"Don't," Andrea pleaded, covering his mouth with her hand. She squeezed her eyes shut to blot out his expression. "You don't know what you're asking of me." She had wanted to be more than a piece of fluff to warm his bed, but this? This was a commitment. How could she give it? Did she even want it? How could he expect her to know now? The questions were endless, each more confusing than the one before.

She lifted her lashes. "I don't know what I want," she confessed awkwardly. "These last few days have been years long. Everything is happening at once and I'm so off balance, I don't even know myself anymore." She stared at him, willing him to understand. "I need time." Slowly she removed her hand. Every muscle in her body tense as she awaited his answer.

For a long moment they faced each other in searching silence. Finally Nick inhaled deeply before dropping a brief, burning kiss on her lips. "I don't want to waste one minute but I'm not going to push you anymore. All I ask is you stay with me as long as you can and as often as you will."

Andrea recognized the importance of his offer by the cost it had demanded of his pride. She could feel the rigid contours of his body where only seconds before there had been a yielding strength. "I want to be with you," she admitted with a deep sincerity.

At her agreement, the tension flowed out of him and he hugged her close. Seconds ticked by as he made no effort to extend his embrace into the pleasurable foreplay they both enjoyed. Andrea gave herself up to the comforting haven of his arms, content to share this silent giving. When he released her with a gentle smile, she returned it with one of her own.

"Come, woman, let's go down and see what Mrs. Guiness left for our lunch." He rose, drawing her to her feet with him. "I'll even tell you about the financial assistance I was able to get set up this morning for Danny and the Dillions."

Nine

——

"That was delicious," Andrea commented with a replete sigh. She drained the last sip of white wine from her glass and surveyed the cluster of empty dishes before her. A drop of the creamy New England clam chowder in a delicate china bowl, a few crumbs of oven-fresh French bread on a plate and a speck of garden-crisp green from their salad was all that remained of their lunch.

"What would you like to do this afternoon?" Nick asked lazily. He grinned at her startled look. "I took the rest of the day off, so what shall we do with it?"

"Sightsee," Andrea replied promptly, without really considering her answer.

"Any place special or will anywhere do?" He held her eyes, enjoying the eager anticipation sparkling in the amethyst depths while she considered the possibilities. Her wish to walk the streets of his city came as no surprise. And he found himself pleased to share her undeniable sense of adventure for the coming expedition.

"There's so much to see. You choose.",

"It's on your head," he warned, getting to his feet and extending his hand to her.

She took it, intrigued by the almost devilish expression on his face. "Where are we going?" she demanded as he tugged her out of the formal atmosphere of the silver- and mint-green dining room to the bold black-and-white tiled entrance hall. "The dishes," she added in protest when it became evident he was actually leaving with her in tow.

"Mrs. Guiness'll get them when she comes back from shopping this afternoon," he explained while locking the door behind them. He tucked Andrea's hand in the crook of his arm as he guided her up the bricked sidewalk. "And to answer your first question, it's a surprise." He chuckled at the rampant curiosity in the look she fixed on him. "I'm not saying a word, except I hope those shoes are comfortable."

Andrea risked a peek at the soft suede boots she normally wore with her jeans. "They are," she murmured, wondering what Nick was going to show her. The barely leashed enthusiasm radiating from him was as contagious as it was unexpected. She couldn't wait to discover their destination.

"I see what you mean about my boots," Andrea groaned good-naturedly two hours later. "If I weren't having so much fun, I'd beg for mercy."

She stared down the long people-crowded docks of Boston's famous waterfront. First built in 1630 as a simple town dock, the harbor grew to more than eighty wharves by the late 1700s. But today the booming seaside area was filled with restored gray granite Green Revival warehouses, shops, restaurants and a medley of museums, as well as the John F. Kennedy Library.

"I swear it'll take days to see this place. I've been here once or twice and I still haven't covered it all."

Nick grinned wickedly. "I know, but it's worth it." He took her hand, removing the sight-seeing pamphlet she had been reading. "One of my favorite exhibits is the brig, the *Beaver II*."

Andrea's brows rose eloquently at the undisguised eagerness in her guide's voice. "I think I'm going to really taste of the flavor of your city this afternoon," she teased, not really minding where they went as long as they were together.

Nick urged her along the dock, easily steering her through the tourists indulging themselves in the historical atmosphere. "Haven't you ever been curious to see an old sailing ship? This one is a replica of one of the three original boats the patriots boarded during the Boston Tea Party. There's even a re-enactment of that evening in the museum adjacent to the ship."

Andrea enjoyed each of the attractions Nick displayed before her. The sights and sounds of a bygone era mixed with the fun and excitement of the modern world with surprising ease. From tea at the Brigg II museum, they moved on to the Children's Museum. Here all the exhibits were touchables, from the appealing City Slice to the Giant Desktop. From there they toured the Museum of Transportation and finally ended with the Gateway to the Sea, a tracing of Boston's three and a half centuries of historic ties with the ocean.

Their short junket was only a sample of the interesting, beautiful and sometimes funny things available in the famous town and Andrea enjoyed every minute of her experience. Nick proved himself to be as insatiably curious about the world as she was herself. It was a pleasure to share her feelings with a man who understood how very special and unique their environment, past and present, was.

Being with Nick heightened the enjoyment. His smile came with a frequency to match her own. Silences became shared experiences of mutual accord. He opened himself to her, allowing her to see another facet of his personality. With the breeze ruffling his hair and playing with the white fullness of his casual shirt, he could have easily been mistaken for a sea captain relishing a short sojourn on land. Only the arrogant swagger and heavy-handed cutlass were missing to complete the picture.

"There's that grin again. What are you thinking?" Nick demanded with lazy amusement. His gaze flickered briefly over her relaxed body before returning to the traffic ahead.

Andrea stretched pleasantly tired muscles while wiggling more comfortably into his Porsche's contoured seat. "How well you fit in with all those ships and docks," she replied, her lips quirking with a teasing smile. "I get the feeling you were probably a pirate in your past life."

He chuckled at the satisfaction in her tone. "No chance. I come from a long line of stuffy lawyers."

Andrea nearly choked on his words. Not too long ago she would have agreed with his self-assessment but not now. "Stuffy?" she gasped, having momentary trouble with her breathing. "I can think of a lot of adjectives for you, but that's not even on the list," she stated with conviction.

"Oh?" he mocked humorously. Taking advantage of a strategically timed red light, his eyes found hers.

The strangely vulnerable need lying just below the laughter sparkling in the aquamarine depths left Andrea's flippant answer unspoken. In a split second all the lighthearted fun flowed out of the afternoon, leaving behind an awareness that bound them together in the midst of a crowd.

"You're a caring man. Tough when you have to be, yet gentle when only a soft touch will do. I watched you with Danny and I saw a part of you beyond the man who disapproved of my life-style. I've seen you struggling to accept me for what I am without the benefit of your own opinions." She stared blindly into his face, knowing she spoke the truth. "You need the challenge of a cause. You like to win against the odds. I think it feeds a need in you like my wandering fills a space in me." The light changed and with it the mood. Andrea shook her head, all too aware of the vague unnamed feelings filling her mind. Feelings she was unprepared to take further at that moment. "Besides, you're one sexy man," she finished lightly.

She purposely ignored the sharply questioning look at her abrupt switch that Nick tossed her way. She was too busy wondering what was happening to her. She had never spoken to a man the way she had just now to Nick. With the voicing of her thoughts, she had suddenly come face-to-face with an inexplicable and totally unexpected realization. She was falling in love with him. The thought should have worried her or, at the very least, made her wish it away. Yet she felt no such regret. Instead, there was a kind of rightness about her knowledge.

Just as beauty was found in the most unlikely places, so too it seemed was love. She hugged her discovery to herself, taking it out at odd moments later to examine it. She showered and dressed, still caught in her own little world. She knew she responded to Nick's conversation during their drive to the restaurant he had suggested for dinner, but she was barely aware of his actual words. The feel of him beside her filled her senses. His scent teased her with memories of the feel of his body against hers, his voice stroked her ears, recalling the deep, dark words of passion he had offered her as she gave him the gift of herself.

"You've been very quiet since we drove home this afternoon," Nick observed, staring at Andrea intently. He covered her fingers as they lay on the highly polished table before them. "Care to tell me what's wrong?"

Needing a moment to think of an answer, Andrea gazed around the softly lit dining room that overlooked the harbor. The tastefully nautical decor created an intimate atmosphere with its carefully placed small booths. But right at that moment she could have wished for something more brightly lit and noisier.

"I was thinking about Danny," she replied, somehow latching onto Scrapper's problem at the last second. The surprise in Nick's expression, followed quickly by a frown, reassured her that he believed her.

He hesitated, searching her face silently. "You don't like the fund I've suggested for Danny and his family?" he asked finally, skepticism evident in his voice.

"Of course I do," she hastened to assure him, knowing his plans were extremely generous. "Through Seven Oaks you've provided the money the Dillions are going to need to get Danny the help he must have. You've even managed to find a way to circumvent their pride by having the foundation administer the account." She spread her hands awkwardly, wishing she knew how to free herself from the tangle of her lie.

"Then what's wrong?"

Andrea glanced down, aware that Nick, with a lawyer's tenacity, was going to keep digging until he had an answer. She gazed unseeingly at her hands with their short nails and slightly calloused palms. She started as Nick's long fingers lightly encircled her wrists. The picture of his elegant bone structure disappearing into the expensive edges of his jacket and shirt cuff was a mute reminder of the differences between them. She was a duck to his swan, a VW to his Maserati, a plow horse to his Thoroughbred; either type was perfect for one of its kind, but mismatched if paired together.

She raised her lashes, recognizing that she had to at least try to explain her doubts. She never got the chance to say a word. The tender look in Nick's eyes stole her objections from her lips.

"Stop fighting us, Flash," he breathed huskily, purposely using her trucker's nickname. His lips twisted at her shocked expression at his perception. "Every time you start comparing my background to yours, I can see it in your face." He tightened his grip, frustrated by his inability to physically wipe away the differences between them. "I can't change who I am any more than you can change who you are. Whether you believe it or not, I wouldn't ask you to now if I could."

Andrea returned the pressure of his hold. Joy flowed through her at the undoubted sincerity of his declaration. "Are you sure?"

He inclined his head, his eyes glittering with honesty. "If I hadn't been, I never would have made you mine. I couldn't have taken a moment of pleasure in our loving if I couldn't accept the person you are. You never were just a body to me," he added with deep conviction.

"But what next?" she asked, impelled by her fear of their future to seek a glimpse beyond the present.

"I don't know," he admitted slowly. For the first time there was an aura of uncertainty about him. "Much as I wish it were different, our careers simply don't mesh and I don't see how we can change it." He studied her, his expression inviting her input.

At the faint though improbable offer of more than just today for them, Andrea felt a surge of hope. Her love made her vulnerable as well as eager for more of him. Yet she had no immediate answer to the problems facing them. She frowned as she considered the alternatives. "I could get Pop to assign me to the local runs," she murmured after a moment. She stifled a sigh at the prospect. Admittedly she had been a little dissatisfied with her nomadic existence recently, but not enough to view the milk runs with any sort of equanimity.

"You'd hate it," Nick stated flatly, easily reading her dislike of the idea. "Besides which you'd still be based in Springfield while I would be here."

She nodded, staring out at the harbor while searching for another solution. "It's too bad you don't have an office in Springfield."

"Or you had a job based in Boston," he countered, doing a little frowning of his own.

"I could try that," she began slowly. "The only problem is I'd lose my seniority. I'd get the trips no one else wanted."

Violet eyes met aquamarine, each pair reflecting a hunger the other recognized. Yet there was a kind of resignation in the eloquent depths which spoke of the acceptance of their realities.

"There has to be a way," Andrea whispered.

He lifted her fingers to his lips, his eyes smiling reassurance across their clasped hands. "I haven't found an unsolvable problem yet. Some just take a little more time to figure out than others."

Andrea stared at him as he kissed each palm, his breath fanning warm tendrils across her skin. "Do you really want me that much?" she asked before she could stop herself. If she had been the blushing type, she would have flamed red at the smoldering look he gave her.

"You're woman enough to know I do," he rasped. He released her reluctantly when the waiter approached with their dinner.

Knowing Nick wanted to be with her as much as she wanted to be with him lent a special poignancy to the evening. Every sense seemed heightened to almost unbearable intensity. It was close to eleven by the time they returned to the town house, yet it seemed like only minutes since they had left.

"Our time is sliding away," Nick muttered as he took her in his arms in the darkened hallway.

Unsurprised by his uncanny voicing of her own feelings, Andrea flowed into his embrace. "Make it stand still for us," she pleaded, knowing she asked the impossible but unable to care.

"Only you can do that," he rasped, pressing her intimately against him. "Give us your three weeks. I'll clear my calendar." The bargain popped out of him without thought, but he felt no regret for asking.

Andrea stared at him, barely able to distinguish his features in the gloom. "All right," she agreed without hesitation. She was bending the rules of a lifetime, risking the comments of those who loved her, but she didn't care. She had to have this.

Tension drained out of him with a deep sigh at her acceptance. He bent his head to cover her lips with his. He had to have a taste of her. It seemed like years since he held her in his arms, felt her body wrap around his like a cloak of living silk. He drank her moan of pleasure and arousal, savoring it like an expensive cognac.

"Nick," Andrea breathed against his lips. She ached for his touch, unashamedly arching into him to demand more. She curled her arms around his neck as he lifted her against his chest and mounted the stairs.

"I think I like carrying you up these steps," Nick murmured huskily, cradling her possessively. "I'll never be able to look at my stairway again without remembering how good you feel in my arms."

He shouldered open his bedroom door, walked over to his bed and laid her gently in the center of the soft pallet. He came down beside her in one fluid movement. He gazed into her eyes trying to pierce the violet shadows visible in the golden pool of light cast by the single bedside lamp left burning.

Andrea lifted her hand to trace the smooth, clean line of his jaw with her fingertips. "So sleek, all bone and muscle," she whispered seductively.

Desire flamed to life in his eyes, turning them into searching aquamarine seas. "Andrea," he groaned as he leaned toward her.

Andrea arched to meet him halfway. Just as their lips fused, the silence was shattered by the shrill ring of the telephone. Andrea jerked back while Nick swore hoarsely. He grabbed the receiver, snapping his greeting with barely restrained irritation.

Andrea sank down on the mattress watching him hungrily. She absently noted the change in the tenor of Nick's responses. But it was the abrupt alteration in his expression that alerted her to listen carefully.

"Don't worry, Helen. Andrea and I'll be right there," he soothed. He paused, his head cocked, then he spoke again. "We'll bring him here and I'll contact the psychologist out at Seven Oaks to see what he suggests. Why don't you pack Danny an overnight bag?"

At the mention of Danny's name and the concern in Nick's voice, Andrea sat up, her passion fading swiftly. Nick hung up and turned to her.

"Danny's very upset. He hasn't eaten all day and he won't play with his cousins. He just sits in the chair where you left him."

"Damn," Andrea swore with unaccustomed vehemence.

Nick drew her against his chest for a second, offering her the comfort of his body. Nothing, he knew, could relieve her mind. "Are you okay?"

She nodded, silently drawing strength from his passionless embrace. After a moment she eased away, forcing herself not to acknowledge the loss she felt when he let her go without a word.

"I guess we'd better leave," she murmured sliding off the bed. "I have a feeling it's going to be a long night."

Andrea had cause to remember her prophetic words during the next few hours. She and Nick arrived at the Dillions to find the situation heartbreakingly apparent. Danny flew into her arms the moment he saw her, clutching her to him with all his strength.

It was surprisingly easy to bundle him into Nick's car and even simpler to bed him down in Nick's guest room. Pathetically eager to please her, now that she had come for him, Danny had obeyed her completely. By the time Andrea joined Nick in the master bedroom, she felt wrung out, both physically and emotionally.

"Is he asleep?" Nick asked the moment he hung up the phone beside the bed.

Andrea padded across to his side, shedding her shoes on the way. He curled his arm around her and drew her down on the mattress as she nodded tiredly. "He exhausted himself, I think. He went out the minute his head touched the pillow."

Hearing the weariness deepening Andrea's voice to a husky whisper, Nick's gaze softened. He tucked her body against his, silently lending her some of his strength.

"I talked to Dr. Fogelman. She'll be waiting for us at Seven Oaks tomorrow morning," he explained quietly.

"Good," Andrea replied with a sigh. "I was afraid we might have anticipated things a bit by bringing Danny here."

"No way," Nick denied emphatically. "Karen was very clear on that score. In fact, she had nothing but praise for the way you've acted since the beginning. Danny, as we all know, has some problems but Karen Fogelman's one of the best child psychiatrists in the state, maybe on the whole east coast."

Andrea raised her head from its comfortable resting place on Nick's shoulder. "I hope he'll be happy at Seven Oaks. I don't think I could bear a replay of tonight." She shuddered at the memory of Danny's rigidly controlled face before he had seen her standing in the Dillion's living room.

Nick tightened his arms around her, absorbing the painful ripples as best he could. "She'll help Danny, I promise you." He lifted her chin with his forefinger until he was gazing into her shadowed eyes. "The Seven Oaks staff has a good record helping traumatized young people. Some have been even worse off than Danny, so try to believe in what they can do."

Andrea stared at him, taking new heart from the utter conviction in his voice. She believed in him and in the foundation he had created and largely endowed with his own funds. She knew, from hearing her brother, Ray, talk, how highly regarded Seven Oaks was.

"I know," she agreed softly. She shook her head, vaguely seeking to dispel the waves of fatigue pouring over her. "I never knew how easy it would be to care about a child, any child."

Nick smiled gently at the surprise in her tone. "They can sure sneak up and capture your heart," he returned. He swung his feet around, drawing Andrea with him to stretch out on the mattress. He wanted her to relax and unwind for a moment before she prepared for bed. The last few hours had been tough and tomorrow in its own way, would probably be just as difficult.

"Wait until Danny says his first word. If you're anything like I was when I saw a child make his first progress, you'll feel like someone just handed you your dearest wish."

He lowered his voice, slowing the tempo of his speech as Andrea settled against his side. He continued talking, recalling a few of the earliest children to benefit from a stay at Seven Oaks. As he spoke, he stroked Andrea's short midnight curls, deriving comfort himself from the inky silken strands beneath his fingers and the sweet warmth of her against him. Her breathing slowed gradually while she leaned into him with increasing weight. He knew by the liquid feel of her body that she was falling asleep, but he couldn't make himself rouse her. She felt so good, so right. Her scent surrounded him, weaving a woman's spell. Her breath whispered against his neck in a delicate feathering pattern that was at once strangely satisfying and oddly stimulating. Desire hovered on the edge of his consciousness, yet a tender possessiveness held him in a more powerful grip.

His woman needed the succor he offered her. For now it was enough. He would be her strength while she replenished herself. He would soothe her body with his touch, her mind with his words. And if his staff could not help the child she cared so much for, he would be there to hold her when she cried.

Ten

─────

Nick, it's beautiful," Andrea breathed, staring at the stately home gracing the grassy emerald knoll before her. "It's far bigger than I thought it would be." She studied the three-storied main house in mellow, aged brick with admiration. From the four white columns guarding a wide raised porch to the beautifully tended grounds cradling its timeless beauty, Seven Oaks radiated a welcome-home charm.

"There are twelve bedrooms in the children's wing," Nick explained, gesturing to the two-storied ell on the left. He eased the car to a stop beside the fountain. It was the focal point of the great circular drive which had once known the splendor of horse-drawn carriages. "The center sections holds the on-staff living quarters, family visiting, music room, library and administrative offices. The right wing is devoted to the common areas used by the children.'' He grinned encouragingly at Danny. Solemn green eyes fixed him with an unblinking gaze.

"The playroom is filled with all kinds of games and toys. There's even a full-scale model train permanently set up in one corner," he added.

Andrea pulled her eyes from the house to glance down at Danny as he pressed closer to her. She took his hand in hers before pointing to a smaller building set a short distance away. "I bet that's where we'll be staying for the next few days," she guessed, infusing her voice with what she hoped was the proper amount of enthusiasm.

It wasn't that she didn't wish to share Nick's apartment over the stables-now-garage, but she wanted Danny to relax enough to give Seven Oaks a chance. So far, he hadn't been actively protesting this new idea in his upset life. But that didn't mean he wanted to be here any more than he wanted to stay with his aunt and her family.

"Let's go meet Karen," Nick suggested smoothly.

Andrea smiled, outwardly conveying a casual acceptance of the introduction between Danny and his doctor. Inside she was a bundle of nerves in spite of the deeply restful sleep she had had the night before. "Okay," she agreed.

Danny scrambled out of the passenger door beside her, still clutching her hand. At that moment, a startlingly attractive blonde in a turquoise jogging suit with a matching band, Indian style, around her head strolled down the stairs. Her deep blue eyes were alight with a warm friendliness impossible to resist.

"'Lo, Nick." She greeted him cheerfully before turning to Andrea with slender fingers outstretched. "He said they were purple, but I thought he was kidding."

Andrea automatically clasped her hand, her surprise at the woman's attitude carefully masked.

"I'm Karen," Karen laughed. "And you're Andrea." She glanced down at Danny, but made no effort to touch him. "And you must be Danny." She swept her arm in a wide arc, indicating a glistening lake in the distance. "The rest of the gang are down at the pond having a picnic under the trees. I was deputized to stay up here and wait for you."

"I don't see any badge," Nick drawled, one brow quirking with assumed confusion.

Karen stared down at her meager chest and the unadorned shirt she wore. "I guess I left it with my horse," she shot back, snapping her fingers.

Nick made a show of looking around. Andrea carefully watched Danny's reaction to their banter. The interest on the small face was faint, but it was there. Silently Andrea blessed Karen Fogelman's unorthodox, but effective approach. She was also glad Nick had warned her to be ready for almost anything.

Within minutes Karen charmed Danny enough to be allowed to hold his other hand. Together the four of them entered the house and turned left down a long corridor filled with doors.

"The kids and I have dubbed this hall the fun house. You never know what's going to pop out when you walk into one of their bedrooms," she explained with a grin.

She exchanged a satisfied glance with Andrea as Danny peered sideways curiously. She opened a door to reveal a room decorated with posters of trucks, models of trucks, a big stoplight for a lamp and a yield sign for a peg board.

"Nick told me how much you like trucks, so I thought you might enjoy sleeping here while you're visiting us."

Andrea tensed at the calm way Karen announced their plans for Danny. Expecting a blowup, she was shocked to see Danny stare first at the psychiatrist, then Nick and finally her. Afraid to move for fear of doing the wrong thing, Andrea remained where she was. She held her breath as he turned slowly and focused on the broad window flooding the room with sunlight. He walked over to study the scene outside. Seconds trickled by like hours before he half faced them again, then nodded slowly, hesitantly. He pointed to the converted stables clearly visible across the yard. The question in his eyes was clear.

"I promise we'll be there for a while," Andrea assured him softly, her lips lifting into a small smile of assurance.

Danny gazed at her mutely, his thin face showing his intense concentration. It was almost as if he were deciding how honest she was being. Out of the corner of her eyes, Andrea saw Nick glance at Karen, receiving an imperceptible nod in return.

"I have an idea, Danny," he announced casually. "Why don't you walk over to the carriage house with Andrea and me while we drop off our suitcases? Karen wants to get back to the picnic before the food's all gone, so she can save us some. Then the three of us will head down to the lake and you can meet the gang." He held out his hand invitingly.

A second passed, then another and another before hesitantly Danny accepted his gesture. The child extended his other hand to Andrea. She felt the beginnings of a natural grin of pure relief curve her lips at his gesture.

"I hope you'll save me an extra large plate, because I'm suddenly starving," she commented cheerfully to Karen.

"How about three large plates?" the psychiatrist replied with a wide smile.

"And three slices of watermelon for dessert," Nick added as they headed back the way they had come.

"Right-o," Karen answered with a jaunty wave as they separated in the main hall.

Feeling more interested in the surroundings now, Andrea glanced around, enjoying the old world elegance of the entrance foyer with its wide staircase curving to the upper floors. "Do you ever regret giving up your family home?" she wondered aloud.

"No," he stated quietly, following her gaze. "The generations of my family were always happy here. But they lived in another era where houses like this were a necessity. Now, Seven Oaks would be more a drain than useful as a private home.'' He shrugged, turning his eyes to hers. ''This way I can live here and the house can serve a purpose at the same time.''

Andrea stared at him, reading the surety in his eyes. No regret lingered in the clear depths, only a peace that came with knowing he had chosen well.

''It's a beautiful home whether it's private or public,'' she murmured softly, her admiration a velvet throb in her voice. For a moment his gaze held hers in a silent exchange of all she had left unsaid. She watched the color of his eyes change, deepening with the rich spectrum of his emotions.

''Let's go show Danny *our* place,'' he suggested huskily.

She nodded, feeling warmed by the way he had shared his home with her. If only it could be possible for them. If only there were a solution to their conflicting careers. But life was full of ''if onlys,'' most of them so futile. Barely aware of Nick shepherding her and Danny across the yard with an easy commentary on the facilities at Seven Oaks, she considered their dilemma once more.

Maybe she could give up her traveling if Nick asked her. Surely her love would soften the blow of losing her freedom. She shook her head, knowing even as she thought it, her idea would never work. She thrived on challenges, of looking beyond the next horizon, of pitting her skill against the unknown.

And Nick would never ask you to give that up, a little voice whispered. Though he still didn't approve of her actual driving, he did understand and accept her motivations. Stalemate. She couldn't quit and neither could he.

"Andrea, are you all right?"

The concern in Nick's voice penetrated her absorption. She blinked, focusing on him. "What?"

He lifted his hand to touch her cheek. "Where were you?"

"Thinking about us," she answered honestly, leaning into his caress.

He frowned at the intrusion of what he preferred to forget. "For the first time in my life, I'm trying to believe tomorrow won't come," he admitted.

Startled at the open confession, Andrea froze. She saw little of the beautiful living room in which she stood, or the silent child a few feet away. The naked vulnerability revealed in Nick's expression held her enthralled. It was as though he had opened a window in his soul to offer her a glimpse of his inner core.

"No more than I am," she whispered, mentally crossing the tiny space separating them to imagine herself in his arms. She could almost feel his warm strength enclose her in a secure cocoon.

Nick pressed his fingers against her skin, aware that with Danny looking on he dare not take Andrea in his arms. He would never be able to let her go without making her his once more. He needed the assuagement her body offered, but more than that he needed the reassurance of being desired by her as if he were the only man she ever wanted. In that moment there would be no clock ticking away precious seconds, no reality standing between them.

He would be man, she woman. Basic, elemental. She was his mate. He wanted no other. He would have no other. Somehow some way, together they would find an answer.

"I love you." Unbidden, the words slipped past his lips to touch hers.

She smiled, her violet eyes suddenly alight with purple fire. "And I you," she replied simply, finding no surprise in his declaration. Though he barely touched her, they had never been closer.

"I could stay here forever," he added, his voice deep with his need. For a heartbeat he drank in the sight and scent of her before he shook himself. He had to remember his audience. He dropped his hand. "Karen'll be waiting for us."

Andrea stepped back, willing herself to ignore the ache unfurling within her. Her body was tense with her desire to give herself to Nick. "Tell me about her," she suggested, latching onto the distraction of the attractive doctor.

"She's married with two college-age girls," he offered after a slight hesitation. "Her husband is a respected surgeon and very much her opposite in personality."

Interested despite herself, Andrea probed delicately. "It must be difficult for them with two such demanding careers," she remarked as they, with Danny between them, descended the outside stairs.

"She admits it gets hectic sometimes, but I doubt that she's ever regretted that part of their life. I know her husband, Doug, doesn't. He's proud of Karen and what she does, just as she is of him.''

"It sounds like they both have a good reason for their feelings." For a fleeting instant she felt a twinge of envy for what the other couple shared. If only she and Nick could find a way to join their lives.

She glanced ahead to the winding path leading to the lake. The youthful enthusiasm of shouting voices seemed to fit the warm sunny day and the sparkling water lying before them. Soothed by the easy atmosphere, Andrea relaxed. She gestured toward a small cluster of adults on a large blanket under the trees near the water's edge. "More of your staff?" she asked, feeling her curiosity about Seven Oaks stir to life once more.

Nick grinned companionably as he took her hand in his. "Yes." He held her fingers lightly in a friendly grasp, knowing his body cried for more, yet willing to settle for this.

"The well-padded, gray-haired lady in the middle is Mrs. Mac, our housekeeper. The tiny powder puff beside her is the girls' housemother and the willowy woman kneeling over the cooler is the boys' room captain. Karen you know, and the other two are our volunteers, Emily and Debbie. Both are local teachers on summer break," he concluded as they came within earshot of the group. "Working hard, I see, ladies," Nick teased.

"Naturally," the women chorused in ragged unison.

"Have you ever known us not to?" the one called Mrs. Mac demanded with mock indignation.

Nick dropped onto the blanket, pulling Andrea down with him. "There's always a first time."

"Not when we know the boss is coming around," the rotund housekeeper shot back tartly amid laughter from her cohorts.

Andrea chuckled appreciatively at the swift reply. "I'm Andrea and this is Danny," she explained a second later. She fielded a shrewd look from Mrs. Mac before she surveyed the array of plastic bowls spread before her.

"Hope you brought your appetites with you," she commented easily. "I don't want to carry any leftovers back to the kitchen." She handed them a plate each, a merry twinkle in her wise eyes. "Dig in."

Andrea wasn't quite sure how it happened, but she found herself doing just as she was told and, oddly enough, so did Nick and Danny. Talk flowed around her, often drawing her in as she expressed an opinion or shared some part of her past.

The afternoon shadows lengthened while the conversation turned to the children spread over the immediate area, playing various games. Even Danny had been tempted from his place beside her to try his hand at fishing with a cane pole with another older boy.

"He looks so normal right now," Andrea murmured, speaking her thoughts aloud. "To see him this way, you'd never believe how upset he was last night."

"It happens like that sometimes," Karen explained gently.

Andrea turned her head to study the other woman's calm expression. "Why can he behave so well with us and not with the family who wants to love him?" Even as she asked the question, Andrea realized the impossibility of her query. As good as Karen was reputed to be, she couldn't know Danny's mind without at least working with him for a while.

Karen shrugged her slim shoulders, not dismissively but in a gesture conveying a multitude of answers. "His aunt may remind him of the mother he no longer has, or it could be she's so different, she feels like a stranger. Then too, the Dillions are responsible for taking him from his home in Williamsburg, so maybe he resents that. Or it could be he can't handle the transition of going from a one-child situation to being one of many." She gazed across the clearing to the small dock protruding into the lake. "As for his speaking, well, my guess is hysterical paralysis brought on by the shock of seeing his parents die."

At the blunt but kindly spoken words, Andrea looked to Nick. For a moment she remembered how upset she'd been when she first learned Danny had been a witness to the crash that had killed his family. "Can you make him well?" she asked quietly, her eyes never losing their hold on Nick's. It helped to know he was there and he loved her.

"With time and care there's no reason to suspect that he won't make a full recovery." Karen paused for a moment before continuing. "His doctor from home agrees with me."

"Good," Mrs. Mac stated briskly, her matter-of-fact voice breaking the small silence that followed Karen's prediction. "It's getting late. We'd best get back to the house so we can clean up." She pulled herself erect with surprising agility for one of her amply endowed girth. She raised her voice to call instructions to her young charges. In seconds the lazy afternoon became a busy hive of activity.

Under the cover of the work going on around them, Nick took Andrea's hand in his.

"Feel better now?" he asked softly, as he rose drawing her to her feet with him.

She nodded, her lips curving into a small smile of relief. "I believed you, you know," she offered. She wondered if she had hurt his feelings by demanding reassurance after all the times he had told her the same thing.

Nick grinned, showing no signs of being annoyed. He dropped a kiss on the tip of her nose. "I know you did, honey."

"Are you two going to stay down here all night?" Mrs. Mac called.

Both turned to see the housekeeper shepherding the last of the children up the path. "Look at that. She's taken Danny with her," Andrea breathed. "I don't think he misses us at all."

"Don't count on it," Nick warned, suddenly serious. "If I've noticed one thing about Danny, it's that he's fine as long as you're close by. But the minute you leave him somewhere, he comes apart.''

Realizing he spoke the truth, Andrea frowned worriedly. "I can't believe I've never noticed." Barely aware of their leisurely walk back to the carriage house, she considered what he'd said. "Is that why you suggested we stay out here for a few days?"

He nodded. "It seemed the wisest course." He leaned across her to push open his apartment door. "Besides, I wanted to show you Seven Oaks. I thought it would interest you if for no other reason than to be sure Danny would be all right here."

Andrea sat down on the oyster-gray and blue sofa, still deep in thought. "I would have been impressed even without Danny," she mused, her gaze somehow focused on the low antique inlaid table before her. "This place is really special. And those women! They couldn't be more different in personalities, yet every one of them seemed exactly right for what they do." She sighed, momentarily wishing she had had even a smidgen of their knowledge when she tried to help Danny.

"What's that sigh for?" Nick asked, drawing her against his side. "Tired?"

She laid her head on his shoulder with a feeling of homecoming. "No, just wishing for the moon for a moment."

"What moon?" He idly stroked the dark curls of her hair feathering along his jaw, hardly aware of the real meaning of their words. He didn't notice that she never answered his question. Instead, he was enjoying the feel of her beside him and the odd contentment filling him just because she was near.

Seconds lingered into minutes as she relaxed against him, lulled by his soothing petting. Quite when the atmosphere began to change, Andrea was unsure. Perhaps it was the light caress of his thumb over the sensitive hollow behind her ear. Or maybe it was the subtle shift of her body so that she faced him fully. Whatever it was, it filled the silence with flickers of heat, tiny swirls of passion to tease the senses.

"You're beautiful, Andrea," Nick whispered huskily, framing her face with his hands.

His lips caressed hers in a sensual brushing, a tasting foray that made her open them with unconscious yearning. Then his tongue plunged into the moist warmth until her mouth closed hungrily on it, sucking and nibbling. She could feel the gentleness leave his arms as he pulled her to him and she welcomed the muscled thrust eagerly. When he tore his lips from hers with a low moan of aching need, she blinked her heavy lidded eyes open dazedly.

"Come to me, love," he rasped, rising with her in his arms. "Share my lonely bed with me. Let me share my heart with you."

Andrea touched his cheek with her hand, her fingers delicately tracing the deceptively slender bones of his face. "Only if I can share my love with you," she replied, taking his lyrically beautiful words and returning them to him with love.

"If it were possible, forever," he agreed, his gaze alive with his desire for her and the passion she gave so freely to him.

Violet eyes met sea-green, each aware that one day tomorrow would come for them. Then without a word spoken, Nick was striding with her to his bedroom where, only today, this moment, mattered.

Eleven

———

I'm going to be late getting back tonight and I'll probably have to come in to town tomorrow as well," Nick announced, a grim edge in his usually liquid voice.

"Problems with the case?" Andrea questioned sympathetically as she pressed the phone closer to her ear. She forced her disappointment from her mind, not wanting to burden him with something he couldn't change. She curled up on Nick's bed, tucking her bare feet under the hem of her dusty-rose robe.

"And then some," he admitted with an irritable sigh. "God, I miss you, honey. The hardest thing I've ever had to do was leave you this morning. If this weren't such a messy case, and a friend—"

"—And a child involved," Andrea pointed out, knowing it was the presence of the small girl caught between two parents that bothered him the most.

"How's Danny doing?" he asked, abruptly switching the subject.

"Far better than I thought he would. Karen had her first session with him this morning. All things considered, she was pleased with his response," she added, unconsciously repeating the psychiatrist's comment.

"How are you faring?"

Andrea heard the change in Nick's voice, the deeper cadence that said more than his actual words. "I'm doing fine if you don't count missing you," she answered honestly, seeing no point in hiding the truth. "Mrs. Mac took me on a tour of the main house in the morning, then I had lunch with the children. After that I got conned into umpiring a mixed group softball game. Those little midgets just about wiped me out. I had to soak in the tub for an hour so I could move again." Nick chuckled appreciatively as she had hoped he would.

"Don't feel bad. The last time I got stuck, I ended up with a shiner and I had a court date the next day." For a moment they shared their laughter, bridging the distance separating them as though it didn't exist. How she had needed to hear his voice, Andrea realized in a flash of self-honesty. It had seemed so simple this morning to assure Nick she would be okay staying at Seven Oaks with him while he drove back to Boston to deal with his unexpected legal problem. After all, it would only be for a few hours, she had reminded herself then and a number of times more during her busy day. Yet in spite of her undeniable and surprisingly intense interest in everything connected with Seven Oaks, she had felt alone.

"Honey, I must go," Nick said ruefully at last. "I should get back about eleven, but if I'm not, don't wait up for me."

Hearing his weariness, Andrea shook her head before he even finished speaking. "Why don't you stay at the town house tonight if you have to work tomorrow, too? It's silly to make the drive out here that late only to turn around and do it again early tomorrow."

Silence greeted her sensible suggestion while Nick thought it over. "Andrea, we have so little time, dammit. I don't want to spend even this much of it apart," he rasped, making no secret of his dislike of the situation.

"Neither do I," she agreed immediately. "But I don't think you need two hours of driving on top of the problem you're dealing with now." She sighed, wanting nothing more than to have him beside her, to feel his arms close around her. But he had a job to do, an important, meaningful job that she wouldn't interfere with. "Please stay in town, darling," she pleaded softly, unconsciously using one of woman's oldest weapons, the gentle word.

"All right," Nick agreed slowly, then added on a rougher note. "But I'm coming home tomorrow night no matter what."

The disgruntled vehemence of his decree drew a faint smile to Andrea's lips. "Sounds good to me," she teased, only half humorously.

Nick grunted before a reluctant grin was born. "Woman, you'd better lay off the softball tomorrow because, when I get back, you're going to need all your energy."

A moment later Andrea hung up the phone, a bubble of laughter in her throat at Nick's threat. Her amusement died almost as quickly as it had come as she surveyed her lonely bedroom. So little time left. Yet it wasn't in her nature to take her pleasure or needs at the cost of others. She knew she had been right to urge him to stay in Boston even if her body ached with an unfulfilled wanting that only Nick could assuage.

Sighing at the foretaste she was experiencing of what it would be like when they parted, she rose, slipped out of her robe and turned out all the lights but one. The soft glow bathed her long naked limbs with gold as she slid into her solitary bed.

Once again her mind sought an answer to their career conflict. She knew herself well enough to realize she wouldn't be content with the part-time relationship that would result if she continued trucking. Yet she would suffocate without something in her life that offered her the challenge and the satisfaction she had always known. She stared at the ceiling, mentally reviewing the few options open to her in the job market. They were depressingly few. If she had had more education, her choice would be far easier. A woman like Karen, for instance, would have little difficulty in changing fields if she so desired.

Disgusted at the bleak picture of their future, Andrea rolled onto her side and turned off the bedside lamp. Instantly she was cloaked in darkness. She gazed into the velvety silence thinking about her and Nick. While they were together, their lives were filled with light, passion and love, but once apart, the light was gone, the passion cold, the love a memory lost in the inky shadows of a far corner of the mind. She had to find a way to make the clock stand still, to alter reality, to capture their wish for a future. But how?

She fell asleep without an answer. Nor did she have one when she awoke to a new, sunny day. The sweet sounds of birds filled the air as she arose. She showered and dressed in her usual jeans, boots and shirt, suddenly determined to seek out Karen Fogelman. Perhaps the older woman might hold the key to her dilemma.

In the short time Andrea had known her, she had come to admire the psychiatrist's intelligence and perception. Perhaps Karen would succeed where she and Nick had failed. At least it was worth a try, she assured herself as she headed up the path to the main house.

Her plans died a swift death when she entered the kitchen to find Mrs. Mac and Emily, one of the volunteers, looking worried.

"What's wrong?" she asked quickly.

"Debbie had an allergy attack last night," Mrs. Mac explained gruffly, a frown on her face. "She and

Emily were supposed to take four of the boys into town to the dentist. Lydia, our room captain, could have deputized for her, but she's taking over Melba's duties so she can take Sandy to have her cast removed.''

Assailed by the complexity of the schedule and the names she had only recently put with faces and duties, it took Andrea a moment to sort everything out.

''I don't know how much help I can be, but I am an extra pair of hands,'' she offered finally.

Mrs. Mac studied her shrewdly before shrugging her plump shoulders. ''Are you sure? The four children going to the dentist are our most difficult boys. That's why they're all going today when the office is usually closed,'' she said bluntly.

Andrea grimaced at the prospect facing her, but she wasn't about to back down. ''Just tell me where we go and what to do,'' she stated quietly.

Mrs. Mac's eyes gleamed with amusement at her resolute expression as she told Andrea what to expect. ''I'm sure you'll do fine,'' she concluded reassuringly.

Andrea wasn't so certain two hours later as she tried to induce her five-year-old charge to sit in the dentist's chair. ''Come on, Tim, she only wants to X-ray your teeth,'' she coaxed, firmly urging the child closer.

She studiously ignored Timmy's horrified facial contortions. The devil glittering in his young eyes told the real story. The little urchin was enjoying himself at two adults' expense. When he literally dug in his heels, Andrea decided she'd had enough. Scooping him up, she plunked him on the contoured vinyl, giving him a warning glare as he attempted to get down.

"You move and I won't tell you one more story about my rig," she promised, meaning every word.

He stared at her assessingly, clearly weighing the strength of her blackmail. "You promised all of us another story if we were good," he pointed out.

She nodded, immediately understanding his reasoning. "So I did. I bet the other guys aren't going to be too happy with you when they find out who messed up in here," she replied, outmaneuvering him neatly. Timmy was the last and quite simply supposed to be the worst of the four. The other three had been reluctant and mostly nervous, but Timmy was out to grab as much attention as he could.

"Okay," he grumbled suddenly, sliding back on his perch with a scowl. "It better be a long story for this stuff," he added, sweeping the young assistant and her equipment with an irritable glance.

Andrea ducked her head to hide a smile. In many ways, Timmy reminded her of Danny. He was a tough guy who only seemed to understand plain speaking. No soft words for those two. Both would probably throw it right back at the unwary.

"How about a mountain blizzard in the Rockies?" She tempted him with a small hint. His expression brightened visibly even as the dental technician began her X-ray routine. He was almost docile, making the procedure pass with an unexpected swiftness that obviously impressed the younger woman.

"Thanks. I don't know how you did it, but I'm glad you did," she whispered as Timmy scooted out of the chair to tell his friends about the story Andrea promised.

Andrea grinned conspiratorially. "I don't know either," she confessed. "If I were gambling, I'd call it beginner's luck."

The assistant's expression conveyed her skepticism. "It looked more like instinct to me. Bet you grew up in a big family."

Andrea shook her head. "No."

"Then you must've done a lot of babysitting."

"No, 'fraid not," she replied, struggling to control her laughter.

Enlightenment dawned. "You're—really—a truck driver?" she gasped, her eyes wide with astonishment.

She nodded. "M'hmm, ever since I passed my driving test." Andrea opened the door to the waiting room with one last glance at the younger woman's dumbfounded face. "I've got a purple truck, too." With that last teasing comment, she entered the small reception area, shutting the door behind her.

"Okay, guys, let's saddle up," she commanded, shifting into her CB lingo. "Mrs. Mac's waiting for us."

"I can't tell you how much we appreciate your help today," Mrs. Mac said seriously. "Not only did you get those scamps to the dentist and back in one piece, but you helped with that gummed up dishwasher, unstuck Maggie's kitten from the tree, settled the fight between Brian and Dickey and found that missing sweeper.

Andrea shrugged her slim shoulders before pushing back a cluster of inky curls off her forehead. "If I'd known you were going to make so much out of so little, I'd have stayed in the carriage house," she muttered, acutely embarrassed. Sitting around a table with four pairs of eyes staring at a person, especially when that person was tired, was not her idea of how to relax over a well-deserved cup of coffee.

"I second Mrs. Mac's opinion," Karen declared firmly. "If you hadn't pitched in, things would have gotten really hectic. In fact, I told Nick that very thing when I spoke to him this afternoon." She lifted her mug to her lips while watching Andrea's reaction closely.

Andrea's lashes flew wide in surprise. "Is he back?"

Karen shook her head. "Still tangled up in that case." She took a slow swallow of the dark liquid. "That's why he called me," she added after a long pause.

"Oh," she breathed blankly, oddly disconcerted to discover how much she disliked hearing about Nick's activities from another woman, even one she admired and respected as much as Karen.

"I don't know about the rest of you, but I'm ready to put my feet up and call it a night," Mrs. Mac remarked, filling the small silence. She glanced at her assistants, Melba and Lydia, to receive a pair of agreeing nods. She rose, followed by her two cohorts. "We'll see you both in the morning."

A moment later Andrea and Karen were alone in the kitchen. Andrea raised her cup to drain the last sip. Nick was going to be late yet again. The hours stretched emptily before her. She was physically worn out from her full day. In a way she had never worked so hard in her life. She should have felt like sleeping, yet she knew only a restless edginess she understood all too well.

"You love him, don't you?" Karen murmured gently.

Andrea met her eyes. "Yes." It never occurred to her to deny Karen's statement or to lie. The calm acceptance of her friend's expression held no surprise.

"I'm glad. I didn't want it to be all on his side."

"You know?" It was she who was amazed, she discovered.

Karen inclined her head, a faint smile curving her lips. "Nick and I have been friends for a long time. He was best man at my wedding and godfather to my firstborn."

Andrea glanced down momentarily, taking refuge behind the screen of her lashes. It was one thing for her and Nick to love each other and share themselves, but were either of them ready for public affirmation?

"Does it bother you that I know?" Karen asked when Andrea made no effort to speak.

"A little," she admitted honestly. "We've barely gotten used to it ourselves."

"If you'd rather not talk about—" Karen began slowly.

Andrea looked up swiftly, suddenly wanting to discuss the situation. "Actually, if you'd like to listen," she probed cautiously, "I do need some input."

Karen studied her thoughtfully. "Your job," she guessed perceptively.

Andrea grimaced. "You got it in one." She spread her hands graphically. "It's the only think I know. I have no college education, no other experience. And doing what I do is certainly not the most helpful thing in a budding relationship. Since I started driving, I've never spent more than three consecutive days at home. Lately, I'll admit I've been less than pleased with my life, but *not* to the point of giving it up."

"Has Nick asked you to?" Karen countered, her eyes demanding the truth.

"No." Andrea gazed at her, marshaling her thoughts. "Being a single nomad is exciting, challenging and frequently satisfying. But being one half of a pair always gone, always alone in a strange place, always missing my mate is an unappealing prospect. If I commit myself to Nick, I want to share my life, my body, my heart and my mind with him. I want him to feel the same."

"What about quality time?"

Andrea rose to pace restlessly to the stove to refill her cup. "If we were just talking about time, I'd agree, but we're not." She focused on the countertop, her back to the older woman. "To run with Nick, to love Nick, I must—even if it's to a limited degree—fold my wings and nest. I don't know if I can do that," she whispered roughly. "I love him enough to leave cleanly before I resent the chains of love that bind me to his side." She swung around, unmindful of the tears welling in her eyes. The sympathy in Karen's expression almost shattered her control.

"What if you had something to fill the place of your traveling?" she proposed carefully, her gaze rock steady. "Something that did all the things for you your life now does?"

Andrea gripped her mug tightly, her fingers whitening with the strength of her hold. "Like what? I'm not bookish, I don't sew, I don't keep house, I'm not musical. The only thing I know is trucking, fixing motors and cooking."

"You left one out," Karen pointed out cryptically.

One black brow rose in puzzlement. "What?"

"You handle problem children with a Pied Piper's magic touch," she answered, as though her ability should have been blatantly obvious.

Andrea walked back to the table, barely aware of even moving. "So?" She sat down to stare at Karen's face.

"So, I've watched you off and on for two days handling minor crises with an aplomb most experienced people never achieve. But what is more amazing than even that is the way you seem to thrive on the complex situations. I'd be willing to bet you enjoy putting yourself against these problem-burdened children. You wade in with one of those outrageous stories and every one of those little devils becomes as meek as any nun would want.''

In spite of herself, Andrea's lips twitched at the humor of Karen's comparison. ''I still don't see the point. Surely you're not suggesting I get a degree and do something in this field. I'm twenty-eight, not nineteen,'' she reminded her bluntly. ''Besides, I don't like school.''

Karen laughed aloud at her vehement disclaimer. ''I could play my career role now and point out that you didn't say the idea held no interest. The only disadvantage seems to be the extra education required.''

Silenced briefly by the accuracy of her observation, Andrea turned Karen's comments over in her mind. Oddly, her first inclination wasn't to dismiss her words out of hand as she would have expected.

She did enjoy the challenge of working with these prickly, often downright obnoxious little people. There was something very special about being able to reach past some unseen barrier to the hurting child beneath the mask. At Seven Oaks a smile and a word held so much more significance than she would have believed possible.

And she had to admit she wasn't restless here, at least not with that I-want-to-see-the-other-side-of-the-hill kind of feeling that had always haunted her. Now, the only edginess she was prey to was the emptiness of her life without Nick to share it. She refocused on Karen to find her watching her intently.

"Think about it, Andrea. You have a very special touch. You can give so much to these children. They need you and I think you need them."

"But education?"

Karen waved the dreaded word away as though it were unimportant. "Night classes if you want to formalize what you do, but if not, you could always work just the way you are. You saw today how much there is to do. There are never enough hands for a labor of love."

Twelve

Andrea couldn't dismiss Karen's solution for some strange reason. It filled her mind with remembered triumphs of the past few days, problems met, smiles given, a special emotion shared. Anger, joy, tears, sadness, they were all there. Love. A labor of love. The doctor's phrase followed Andrea back to the carriage house.

She automatically reached for the light switch as she entered, before realizing the living room was lit by the two lamps flanking the sofa. She blinked, startled, as the sound of running water drifted down the hall leading to the bedroom and its adjoining bath.

"Nick," she whispered, her earlier fatigue dissolving on knowing he was back. She padded quickly through the apartment, barely pausing at the partially closed bathroom door. She almost collided with Nick when he emerged just as she entered.

"Andrea." His eyes lit up at the sight of her. Unmindful of his wet body, he held out his arms and she walked into them. "I missed you, woman," he murmured deeply.

Andrea touched his face with light fingers, blindly reacquainting herself with the feel of him. "Why didn't you come up to the house?" She was surprised to note the faint reproach in her question.

Nick noticed it too, his lips crooking wryly. "I started to, but I was beat and I needed to clean up a bit," he replied, his gaze roaming possessively over her.

For the first time Andrea saw the deep lines of exhaustion around his eyes and mouth. "Is everything all right?" she asked, content, now that he was here, just to be held in his arms.

He nodded. "For a while." He bent his head to kiss her with tempting lightness. "But I don't want to talk about my work or anything else at the moment," he breathed against her lips.

"Neither do I, really," she drawled back seductively. She ran her fingers slowly over his damp shoulders. "You're wet."

"I know. Do you mind?" His mouth covered hers before she could answer, this time stealing into the moist cavern for a swift taste of her. He withdrew, his gaze challenging her.

She met his look with a dare of her own. "No, in this heat you'll dry in no time," she promised. She arched against him, reinforcing her provocative comment with her supple body.

Desire turned his aquamarine eyes more green than blue. Her boldness was a vivid reminder of the dreams of her he had carried with him the last two days. "Keep that up and we won't make it to the bed," he warned. His head lowered and each word was a stinging kiss on her waiting lips. "My control where you're concerned is nonexistent." He met her eyes, his expression tight with his need and a strange gravity. "I don't think I'm going to be able to let you go. I think I'd rather survive sharing your life whenever you'll come to me than never having you again."

Andrea studied him anxiously. Could he really mean it? Could he really accept a part-time love? Could she? In that second she knew she could. She would take what they had and be grateful for the strength and the generosity of their love. Whatever the obstacles, Nick was the man she wanted. Tomorrow would come. It wouldn't be perfect. It wouldn't be what either of them really wanted. But they could make it enough.

"Make love to me, Nick," she whispered. "Be mine and I'll be yours."

Nick crushed her to him, needing no second urging to take what his body and his heart ached to know once more. He lifted Andrea in his arms to stride confidently to their bed. He laid her down, knowing as he gazed at her delicately strong face he would risk anything to share his life with her. "Marry me," he commanded, his words more a plea than the order that they sounded like. "Be my wife as well as my love."

Andrea stroked his cheeks, her fingers trailing lightly over his lips as he awaited her reply. "I would give it up for you if you asked," she said instead.

He inhaled sharply, recognizing the measure of her commitment to him in her offer. For a second, he wanted to accept the temptation. Selfishly, he wanted her always near. He wanted to be there for her if she needed him. He wanted to banish the lonely hours apart that lay in their future.

"I'll never take from you what isn't mine to have. You love your life. It made you who you are." He gently began to undo the buttons of her shirt. "Run free if you must, just as long as you come home to me. I'll always be waiting for you."

Tears gathered in Andrea's eyes at the vow that flowed from his lips with so much emotion. She slipped her arms around his shoulders, raising herself to him. She barely noticed her blouse floating away as she covered his lips with hers. She could wait no longer. She needed him, wanted him, with every fiber of her being.

He came to her, his lips meeting hers with an urgency to equal her own. His hands drew patterns of flame over her skin, searing away the rest of her clothes.

Her flesh warmed, her body melted into his like molten honey. His dark words of passion filled her senses. Some were as beautiful and lyrical as poetry, others as graphic and bawdy as only a man's man can be. Yet it made no difference, for every liquid note touched Andrea, arousing her beyond anything that had gone before.

Just when she was certain she could stand no more, the words ceased. Instead, Nick's labored breathing harmonized with hers as together they began the journey into the challenging realm of that final lovers' paradise. Across the roadway of their minds and bodies, through the intimate shadowed valleys, they rode ever closer to the summit. It was a golden odyssey begun in sunset and completed in a glorious sunrise. Color and light exploded, creating an ending to the night and a beginning of a new day. Their day, their future.

Arms entwined, they lay spent, yet exhilarated. "If all our separations end like this, I could get quite addicted," Nick rasped. His hands went to cup her buttocks to cradle her closer to him.

Andrea laughed breathlessly, her arms tightening around him. "You don't think it might get repetitious?" she teased. She gasped as he suddenly flexed inside her. "Stupid question, I see."

He rolled over to face her, their bodies still linked intimately. "Damn right, woman. You couldn't be repetitive if you tried." He nuzzled her throat, his hands moving to stroke her breasts. Lowering his head, he saluted each pink tip before cuddling her closer. "Rest, wife-to-be," he whispered. "We both need it."

* * *

Nick glanced across at Andrea, his lips lifting into a smile to mirror hers. "Glad to be heading back to Boston?" he teased gently.

Andrea shook her head, while settling more comfortably into her seat. "Not really. These last four days have been a real education." She laughed aloud, recalling the final two she and Nick had spent helping out together. "That was a very professional looking swing you built for the girls."

"It was easier than getting involved in that cutthroat basketball game you and the boys were playing," he shot back with a reminiscent grin. "You wore them out so much that, for once, they went to bed without a murmur."

They exchanged a long look before Nick turned his attention to the empty road ahead. Silence filled the minutes with quiet companionship before Nick spoke again.

"Karen tells me Danny's finally beginning to open up," he remarked, satisfaction evident in his voice.

"I know. I had a talk with her about him before we left this morning."

Nick flicked her a quick glance. "Was that all you discussed?"

Startled at the unexpected question, Andrea hesitated. So far she hadn't mentioned Karen's suggestion for her future to Nick. Maybe she should have, yet, even now, she couldn't bring herself to offer him a hope that might turn out to be false. While Karen's ideas had lost much of their improbability, she still wasn't sure they were truly a viable alternative.

"Andrea?" Nick prompted, when she made no effort to answer. "Is something wrong?"

Pushing her thoughts aside, Andrea gave him a reassuring smile. "No, I was just thinking I should call Pop and let him know I'm engaged," she countered, improvising quickly. She lifted her left hand to survey the amethyst-and-diamond ring she wore. "I'll bet he'll be surprised."

Diverted by her obvious pleasure at the prospect, he missed the abrupt change of subject. "I'm not so sure. Your father's a very shrewd man and he knows you very well."

Andrea frowned with mock indignation. "I'm unpredictable, remember?" Her eyes danced with mischief as she watched a smile curve his lips. "At least that's what you told me when we took that herbal bath at three this morning." She chuckled at the faint red tint to his skin.

His glance swept her relaxed figure, promising a delicious retribution. "Don't believe everything you hear about staid Boston lawyers, my love," he shot back, goaded.

Andrea slid over as close as the console shift would allow. She leaned against his shoulder, her lips only a breath away from his ear. She blew gently against the vulnerable, and on him, highly sensitive spot.

"I take back every dull name I ever called you," she whispered throatily. She felt the shiver of response ghost through him with a sense of feminine power. "I had no idea of the things an inventive person could do in the shower."

Nick groaned audibly, his hands tightening on the steering wheel. "If you don't move over on your side of the car, you also might find out just how creative I can be in a natural setting," he growled meaningfully.

Laughing, Andrea did as he suggested. She wiggled around in her seat once more and leaned back to enjoy the ride home. The miles rolled by, unbroken by words. Sunlight flickered through the trees, dappling the highway with a multitude of shadows. It was a beautiful day. A space out of time filled with harmony, peace and an almost perfect feeling of completeness. The increasing traffic as they entered the city limits did little to disturb Andrea's mood.

But there was an added element when she and Nick mounted the steps to his front entrance. A sense of homecoming so sweet, so unexpected surged through her. Soon this would be her anchor, her place to rest. She watched Nick as he closed the door behind them, aware as never before of what Nick meant to her. He swung around, his eyes meeting hers.

"Welcome home, Andrea," he said huskily, moving to take her in his arms.

It was as natural as breathing for her to meet him halfway, her lips parted to invite his kiss. She melted against him as he accepted her offer, her arms going around him to bind him to her. His tongue stroked the soft inner tissue, enticing hers into the love duel they enjoyed so much. Seconds slipped by as reality faded and passion reigned supreme.

Suddenly the doorbell shrilled, shattering the exquisite delights they had just begun to sample. Nick lifted his head, his breathing sounding harsh in the stillness. A frown darkened his face as he turned to stare at the closed panel.

"Who the devil is that?" he muttered just before another irritating peal intruded.

Andrea was no more pleased with the interruption than he was. She pushed gently against his chest. "I don't know, but whoever it is, they're getting impatient."

Nick released her reluctantly. He opened the door abruptly, temper turning his eyes to stormy seas. The sight of a visibly distraught woman clutching the hand of a whimpering child made him control his annoyance.

"Margaret, what are you—"

He got no further as his uninvited visitor edged past him with her child in tow. "He was going to take Tammy away for good. I just know it. That trip to the park was just a ruse," she rushed on tearfully. "I couldn't stay...."

After the mention of the names Margaret and Tammy, Andrea barely heard the emotional outpouring. This had to be Margaret Greer, the woman Nick was representing in a divorce action and also the reason he had come back to town Wednesday and Thursday. No wonder he had described her as overwrought and living on her nerves. She looked ready to break. Her daughter was a damp replica of her mother. Andrea's heart softened at the bewildered pain in the intense little face. Six years old was entirely too young to be forced to cope with the problems of her parents.

"Why don't I take Tammy into the kitchen for a snack?" Andrea suggested the moment Margaret Greer paused to get a breath. She smiled at the child. From the corner of her eyes, she saw Nick's client hesitate, then look to Nick for guidance.

He nodded slightly. "This is Andrea Carpenter, my fiancée," he explained quietly. He knelt down, gently separating Tammy's fingers from her mother's. "She's a very special lady and she likes little people best of all."

Andrea waited, hoping Nick's support would overcome Tammy's justifiable reticence. She held her breath as solemn blue eyes studied her intently. She ached to hug her close as the small bottom lip trembled, then steadied.

"Okay," she whispered, letting Nick place her hand in Andrea's.

Being careful not to startle the girl, Andrea guided her through the dining room to the kitchen. Working on a technique she had seen one of the volunteers use with an upset charge, she began a soft monologue about things that might appeal to a six-year-old. She was amazed at how much she had picked up during her stay at Seven Oaks.

She and Tammy laid a table for two with cookies and lemonade. They were halfway through the snack before Andrea was rewarded with her first smile. It was wobbly and decidedly brief, but it was there, she assured herself, feeling a deep sense of satisfaction at having soothed the small creature, if only for a moment. A labor of love, Karen had said, and she had been right.

Suddenly, like a giant puzzle with the one missing piece found, she realized her wandering was over. Here was where she belonged. Here with her man and the work he had begun. There was so much she could do. So many ways she could find the challenges, the personal satisfactions that were so important to her nature. How often had there been a child in need with no one to hear? How often had Nick tried to help with no one to share his thoughts, his hopes or his despairs? No longer. This was her place now. Determination crested on a wave of exhilaration. She could hardly wait to tell him of her decision.

At that moment Nick, with Margaret beside him, appeared in the doorway. Their eyes met across Tammy's head. Somehow he must have seen something in her expression, Andrea realized as she gazed at him. A strange light flickered in the ocean cool depths, bringing heat and life. She rose, forcing herself to acknowledge Margaret Greer's thanks and Tammy's goodbye. As she walked beside Nick to the door, she was conscious of the tension in the arm circled around her waist. She barely managed a smile as she watched the mother and daughter leave.

"What's going on?" Nick demanded the moment they were alone once more. "Talk to me. Tell me what you're thinking."

Andrea turned in his arms, her eyes soft with tenderness. The uncertainty in his voice touched her deeply, making her aware more than ever of his vulnerability and her own.

"What would you say if I quit my job?" she asked, watching him closely.

Nick inhaled sharply, caught completely unprepared by her serene tone. "We've discussed that," he pointed out carefully, feeling something swirling about him that he didn't understand.

"Do you think I'm good with your children?" she queried, reframing her question.

"You know I do and so do a lot of other people." His hands tightened on her slender curves as he began to suspect what was coming.

Andrea arched nearer, her lips lifting into her faint smile at his obvious restraint. She was teasing them both with her slow approach, but somehow she couldn't seem to stop herself.

"Karen and I've been talking," she murmured, lightly stroking the nape of his neck.

Nick stared at her, reading the mischief in her extraordinary purple eyes. Relief filled him because suddenly he knew. Karen's hints, Mrs. Mac's praises, memories of the last week all combined to create a future he hadn't dared dream would exist.

A reckless grin slashed his lips as he bent and scooped his woman into his arms. "Have you now?" he drawled blandly as he mounted the stairs.

Andrea giggled engagingly. He guessed, darn him. "Mm hmm." She traced the outline of his lips with her forefinger. "She says I'm a natural. So does Mrs. Mac. The children like me."

Nick entered his bedroom and strode to his bed. "And?" he prompted, cradling her tenderly in his arms.

"And would you like an ex-nomad with a flair for handling cookie-crunching, knee-scraping little urchins sharing your life on a permanent basis?" she breathed, her voice deepening seductively with every word. "Or would that be too repetitive for a very unpredictable Boston lawyer?"

Slowly Nick eased her to her feet, without allowing the smallest space to come between them. "Do you mean this, my love?" he demanded with husky insistence. "Do you really want to change your life this much?"

Andrea framed his lean face with her hands. She stared into the beautiful sunlit seas of his eyes. "I really want this, not only for what it will mean for us, but for what it means to me. Children like Danny, Tim and Tammy deserve to have someone there. They ask so little and give so much. A smile of joy to rival a desert sunrise, a tear of happiness with the clarity of a diamond. But best of all it's the pure, uncomplicated love in those small bodies. They're so generous, so unbelievably honest. I want to share, learn from it and give to it if I can.''

Nick raised his fingers to her cheeks to gently trace the slender silver trails of moisture from her eyes. ''Welcome home, love,'' he whispered simply, his expression holding a rainbow of emotions just for her. He folded her into his arms, his mouth covering hers. Their lips met, sweet breaths mingled while two hearts beat as one.

His gypsy woman had found her place to rest at last. Her wandering was done. She was his forevermore.

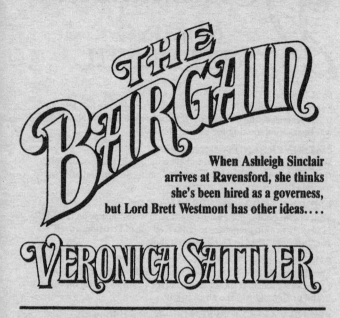

 *Silhouette Desire*

COMING NEXT MONTH

#361 MADE IN AMERICA—Jo Ann Algermissen
Sunny Peiper always had the last word. When Blayne had left her seven years ago, she'd shouted, "I *could* be pregnant!" Now, Blayne was back—and looking for Blayne, Jr.

#362 SILVER SANDS—Robin Elliott
When Cam Porter was called to help a damsel in distress, he didn't realize he'd been cast as the knight in shining armor. But after meeting Lisa Peterson, he wasn't complaining.

#363 JUST GOOD FRIENDS—Lucy Gordon
Toni and her not-quite-ex-husband Flynn were "just good friends." However, working together re-ignited all the old passions, until friendship was the last thing on their minds.

#364 NEVER A STRANGER—Marcine Smith
Shea had come to Favor's rescue when she'd become trapped on a barbed-wire fence. It didn't take long for Favor to realize that Shea's brand of first aid was the all-over kind.

#365 NO WALLS BETWEEN US—Naomi Horton
When Marc d'Angelo broke a gaping hole through Paige MacKenzie's living room wall, she was understandably furious. But one look at Marc and Paige knew her life would never be the same.

#366 MINX—Jennifer Greene
Even if Grant helped Kathryn free the "inmates" of her inherited mink farm, he knew that she was one minx his heart wouldn't let go.

AVAILABLE NOW:

ATTRACTIVE, SPACE SAVING BOOK RACK

Display your most prized novels on this handsome and sturdy book rack. The hand-rubbed walnut finish will blend into your library decor with quiet elegance, providing a practical organizer for your favorite hard-or soft-covered books.

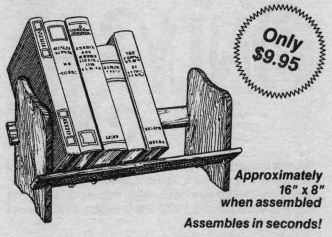

Only $9.95

Approximately 16" x 8" when assembled

Assembles in seconds!

To order, rush your name, address and zip code, along with a check or money order for $10.70* ($9.95 plus 75¢ postage and handling) payable to *Silhouette Books*.

Silhouette Books
Book Rack Offer
901 Fuhrmann Blvd.
P.O. Box 1325
Buffalo, NY 14269-1325

Offer not available in Canada.

*New York residents add appropriate sales tax.

BKR-2R